DOUBLE DOUBLE RECOIL & TROUBLE

PAIN IN THE ASSASSIN MYSTERIES 2

ADDISON MOORE

BOOK DESCRIPTION

An assassin who works for the mob. One hot detective.
And a killer. Living in Honey Hollow can be murder.

Cosmopolitan Magazine calls Addison's books, "...easy, frothy fun!"
Humor with a side of homicide.

A laugh out loud standalone cozy mystery by New York Times,
USA TODAY, *&* Wall Street Journal *bestseller Addison Moore*
A MURDER IN THE MIX SPINOFF!

Includes RECIPE!

My name is Eufrasia Canelli, but everybody calls me *Effie.* **I come from a big Italian family with big hearts, big appetites, and an even bigger bankroll that's cleverly hidden from the IRS.**

I'm not married to the mob, I was born into it. Just last year, I was laid off from my career at a tech company and in an effort to keep from moving back home—I went crawling to the biggest crime lord I know—my Uncle Jimmy.

He gave me two options: Dance at his strip club—or hunt down his enemies.

Seeing that I'm no fan of public nudity, I opted for murder.

Let's just say my mortality rate so far is nil.

Okay, so I'm not a straight shot, but my Uncle Jimmy doesn't seem to mind and I'm still raking in enough money to keep a roof over my head.

I also took a part-time job at a local bakery. Not only do I get to satisfy my sweet tooth for free, but I get a decent cover when I'm asked about my employment.

My uncle has a new assignment for me—one that I would do anything to get out if I could. But as it stands, my own neck is on the line. To complicate matters, my uncle has given me yet another hit for the haunted month of October. It's double for my trouble and my luck is just about to run out.

To top things off, a body turns up at a spooky restaurant called the Tavern of Terror and you won't believe who's sitting on top of the suspect list. At this point I'd welcome a hot date with the boogie man.

I guess it's true what they say—living in Honey Hollow can be murder.

CHAPTER 1

Four hours from now…

The Killer

The back alley is as dark as it is bitter cold. And both remind me of my heart at this moment.

The icy fall air blows the leaves that have fallen from the neighboring oaks, leaving them rattling around in the wind like the bones of a skeleton. Spooky season is upon us, and that seems appropriate because things are about to get downright terrifying for my target.

I watch from the shadows as they approach, unsuspecting of the danger lurking nearby. It's almost poetic the way fate has brought us together in this dimly lit place—a back alley, where so many of our dealings have taken place.

They stop in their tracks. I can tell they're sensing a presence but unable to identify where it's coming from. The fear emanating from them is palpable, their breaths quickening as they struggle to wrap their head around the situation.

"Hey?" They stagger my way, squinting in a feeble attempt to make me out. "What the"—they stop short once they spot the weapon in my hand. There's no point in hiding it. There's no point in hiding what's about to transpire.

"You?" they sputter in disbelief. "You're going to do this to me, of all people?"

I step forward and revel in the power I hold over them. The moonlight glints off the gun in my hand, casting an eerie glow on their face.

"I'd say it's nothing personal—that it's just a matter of circumstance, but I think we'd both know that was a lie."

They take a step back and their eyes dart around the alley for any chance of escape. But there's no escape from the web they've woven. They're trapped—caught in the clutches of their own demise.

"What did I ever do to you?" they plead as desperation seeps into their voice. "This is a mistake."

"Mistake?" A dark laugh ripples through me. "This is no mistake. You see, life is full of choices and you've made yours. Now it's time to face the consequences."

Their eyes widen as the weight of their actions crash down over them. They struggle to find words as their breathing grows shallow.

This is it.

The final meet-up of predator and prey. The final act in a wicked game that's gone on far too long.

"*Please,*" they beg, their voice laced with regret. "Give me a chance to make it right. I can change. I swear."

I tilt my head, considering their plea. But mercy has no place in this dark alley or in my heart.

"It's too late for redemption, buddy," I say, stepping closer with each word. "You rolled the dice and now it's time for you to meet your maker."

Their body seizes as they realize the inevitability of what's to come. And in their eyes, I see a reflection of my own darkness.

Without hesitating, I fire a shot, then two to make sure I get the job done right.

I watch as their body crumples to the ground, and just like that, my heart pounds with a shred of remorse. I high-tail it out of there and back into the harsh reality as the world moves on, oblivious to the tragedy that just unfolded.

And as I fade back into the darkness, I carry the weight of the life I extinguished.

It's a burden I must now bear forever.

CHAPTER 2

Present

Effie

"*L*et me have him," Niki demands just this side of a whine, her eyes sparkling with enough mischief to make any court jester jealous.

I prop myself against the gleaming counter, right here at the Cutie Pie Bakery and Cakery with my arms crossed, tapping my foot impatiently as my little sister does her best to get under my skin. It doesn't take much these days. And Niki is sort of a pro at it.

"Cooper is my kind of trouble," she goes on. "Tall, dark, and dangerously good-looking. I'm an expert at reeling in men like him. It's a shame to let him go to waste and we both know it."

I roll my eyes at the thought. "You're an expert at something, all right," I grunt. "Last time I checked, Bruno the butcher had a restraining order against you. Let's just say you have a way of scaring off potential suitors faster than a haunted house on Halloween night."

She shoots me a devilish grin. "What can I say? My sizzling charm can be overwhelming for some folks. But Cooper? Dear ol' Coop won't be able to resist my irresistible self. I'll have him eating out of the palm of my hand like a zombie devouring fresh brains. Besides, he deserves a proper sendoff and we both know it."

"*Geez.*" I swat a dishtowel her way as if I were swatting a bug. "Would you keep it down?"

Speaking of Halloween, it's the middle of October and all things spooky have taken over our small town of Honey Hollow. The bakery has enough witches, ghosts, and goblins scattered around that it practically qualifies as a haunted house itself. But it's the scent of freshly baked cinnamon rolls that assures our customers they're in the right place.

The bakery might be decorated to the hilt for this spooky, kooky month and all of its haunted charm, but I'm not feeling all that charming these days.

My name is Eufrasia Margarita Canelli, but people just call me Effie. I'm five feet five inches of fun, have dark medium-length hair, dark eyes, and a knack for landing myself in the deadliest and some might say darkest situations. Like with Cooper.

"You are under no circumstances to give Cooper Knox a proper anything," I hiss over at my look-alike. Niki and I have three other siblings as well, and each one of us Canelli kids is a mirror of the other—chocolate dark hair, coffee brown eyes.

What can I say? We're delicious. Not to mention the

fact my parents were one-hit wonders when it came to the genetics department.

Niki leans in as customers swarm around her. "You mean Cupertino Knox Lazzari, aka your next *hit*." There's a tiny gleam in her eyes as she says those words and it only confirms what I've long suspected. My sister is a psychotic loon—another genetic trait my parents are responsible for.

But as it turns out, she speaks the truth.

About a year ago, I was let go from the tech sector, and in an effort to keep a roof over my head, I went crawling to my Uncle Jimmy for a job. He gave me two choices—dance on stage at his strip club or take up arms and go after his enemies.

Suffice it to say, I was fitted with a Glock.

And my next hit? Cupertino Knox Lazzari—aka Detective Cooper Knox. His crisscrossed moniker is a story for another time.

The long and short of it?

The Lazzaris and the Canellis have been the primary warring mob families in this part of Vermont going as far back as the *Mayflower*.

Okay, so maybe not that long, but it sure as heck feels like it.

And by the looks of it, my Uncle Jimmy is ready to initiate another deadly round of that turf war, starting with the only man I've had feelings for since I fell in love with Marty Hindberger's peach fuzz on his upper lip back in seventh grade.

But I'm not in seventh grade anymore. I'm barreling toward thirty and I've got a bullet lodged in my weapon just waiting to burst out and give Cooper the kiss of death that my uncle thinks he deserves.

Let's get one thing straight. I've yet to send any one of my uncle's foes to paradise, or the hot place either for that matter.

My motto is *I maim to please*, and Uncle Jimmy hasn't said squat so far, because as it turns out, each one of those goons he's sent me after has owed him quite a bit of money. And after I've landed a bullet in a stray limb, surprise *surprise*, they've all paid my uncle back with interest.

But the hit on Cooper just so happens to be different. Not only does Cooper not owe my uncle a dime, but my uncle wants him dead as a doornail for the simple fact Cooper has become a nuisance to him.

Honestly? I have a feeling I'm on the cusp of achieving the very same feat.

A few of the customers burst into laughter as they wait for their sweet treats while my coworkers, Suze and Lily, work busily to meet their needs.

I sigh past my sister as I take in the bakery in all its Halloween-inspired glory. The walls are painted a buttery yellow, the scent of freshly baked chocolate chip cookies makes my stomach growl, and there are enough spiderwebs, skeletons, and pumpkins to make any cemetery jealous.

Spooky decorations dangle from the ceiling, casting eerie shadows on the walls while eyeball-shaped desserts beckon from the display case, daring customers to take a bite. And that they do. We can't seem to keep any of the scary, hairy desserts in stock.

Lily Swanson, a dark-haired cutie, bounces this way, reeking of attitude. She's worked here far longer than I have but has welcomed me with open arms—albeit those arms of hers are more like claws. She's been known to be a bit catty. And honestly, it's what I like best about her.

"Well, well, well," she coos. "What's got the two of you all hot and bothered?" She smirks as if she's about to win the gossip lottery.

I like Lily. She's not only sassy to a fault, but she happens to share my penchant for glazed crullers. Lucky for us, the owner of this place, Lottie Lemon, lets us eat our weight in just about any dessert we like.

My part-time job here at the bakery is more or less a ruse, but one that I'm afraid Cooper is on the brink of blowing up—thus the real reason I've been instructed to blow *him* up.

In other words, my uncle thinks the handsome detective is starting to smell the mobster blood in the water—thus the next drop of blood is required from the handsome detective himself—via my bullets and me.

How did I get tangled up in this mess again?

Oh, that's right, *greed*. That is, if you can call a desire to pay your rent greedy.

"I'm trying to steal her man," Niki offers Lily a *greedy* grin to go along with the explanation.

"Cooper is not my man," I'm quick to offer up without so much as a thought.

I shoot Niki a dirty look for making me say those words. So much for keeping things close to the vest. But I suppose as long as we don't talk bullets I can evade an arrest. Lily has no clue what I really do for a living and I'd like to keep it that way.

"Oh, honey"—Lily gives a throaty laugh in my sister's direction—"only a fool would give away a man of that caliber." She nods right at me. "I saw that kiss you shared at the fall festival. He's not going anywhere."

I make a face. "Yeah, well, that kiss was weeks ago and it's yet to be repeated."

Suze struts over.

Suze Fox is an older woman, a tough cookie with short blonde hair. Scratch that, mostly *gray* hair and a perpetual scowl. She's Lottie's mother-in-law or ex-mother-in-law, or some sort. Either way, Suze can't really stand Lottie despite the fact Lottie signs her paychecks. Suze is basically a crabby old lady who everyone tolerates because she doesn't mind working the rush hour.

"Are you two at it again?" Suze winks my way. "Fighting over a man like he's the last piece of candy in the trick-or-treat bag? Let me tell you, men are about as fun as a haunted house. But Halloween candy? Now that's worth the fuss." She reaches past me and snags a fun-size candy bar from the witches' cauldron full of treats we have set out for the customers. "Especially these chocolate patties filled with peanut butter. I just can't get enough. And at this time of year, I allow myself to gobble down a bag a night!"

Now that's living.

Niki scoffs at the woman. "Suze, you'd be singing a different tune if you tasted the testosterone treats I have. Trust me. There are plenty of men that are worth the tasty battle. And when you find the right one, it's like finding a full-size candy bar in your loot bag. Pure delicious ecstasy."

Suze bursts out with a laugh. "Oh, Niki, I've been around this planet twice as long as you have and I can attest to the fact none of them are worth the trouble. We've got Halloween right around the corner, and the only kind of candy I need comes in the form of bite-size chocolates and caramel apples. No man can compare to the sweetness of a perfectly crafted confection. Have I mentioned the peanut butter patties?"

Niki lifts a brow my way. "I bet there's nothing bite-size about Coop."

"Good grief," I groan as I quickly grab a miniature candy bar for myself, and it just so happens to be a Reese's peanut butter cup. The best of the best.

I just may be on the fast track to becoming a crabby old lady myself. Gobbling down a bag of these beauties a night doesn't sound like such a bad deal.

"I think you're right about Cooper." Lily nods to Niki as she grabs a handful of candy to appease her sweet tooth. "That man is a full-size hunk of handsome. I'm just glad I'm not single anymore. I've got a man who sets my heart racing like a runaway train. Just wait until you find the perfect man, Niki. You won't have to lust so hard after Effie's main squeeze."

Suze shakes her head. "Oh, come now. That's like finding the perfect costume to wear on Halloween night in a sea of polyester nightmares. We all know it's not possible. Especially not this time of year. All of the freaks come out of the woodwork, and the next thing you know some stranger with fangs is asking to suck the blood out of your toes."

"No one wants to hear about your foot fetish, Suze." Lily waves her off. "Bloodsucker or not, it's about finding that one guy who's a treat, even amidst all the spooky tricks."

Suze huffs her way, "Tricks, treats, who needs 'em? I'd rather have a plate of salted caramel apple pie and a good cozy mystery to read. Men may come and go, but pie, now *that's* forever."

"*Hear, hear,*" I sing. Because is there anything more truthful than pie?

"And let's not forget, girls," Suze croons. "We've got a bakery to run. There's magic in these sweet treats, and they are far tastier than any man. We have the power to whip up confections that make people swoon. Who needs a man when we can work our magic with cupcakes and cookies? We're like modern-day sorceresses of baked goods."

That might confirm Lottie's theory about Suze being a powerful witch.

"Forget about the baked goods," Niki snips. "Let's talk bodies—as in dead bodies. Who do you think will stumble upon the first stiff of the season? Lottie or Effie?"

A hard groan comes from me.

It's true. Both Lottie and I have stumbled upon a few corpses, but let's call a deadly spade a spade—Lottie can dance circles around my corpse-finding skills. She's sort of gone pro herself.

"I'll go first." Niki shrugs. "My money is on Effie. She's got a talent for finding trouble even when it's disguised as a harmless pumpkin spice latte." She holds up her coffee as if to prove her point. "She spilled one all over her laptop last week."

Darn right, I did. And now I'm in the market for a new laptop—and maybe a new favorite beverage. I still haven't forgiven it for the malfeasance.

Suze chuckles with a demented gleam in her eyes. "Effie may have the grace of a one-legged vampire on a pogo stick, but Lottie? She's got the luck of a black cat on Halloween night. My bet is on her to stumble upon the first body. And believe me, she'll be on it like it's the last piece of chocolate in a haunted candy jar."

"I heard that," Lottie says, strutting this way, her caramel curls bouncing over her shoulders. "All right, it's true. I'm living my worst nightmare. I'll admit, I have a knack for attracting chaos like a moth to a jack-o'-lantern, but let's not forget, Effie has her own special talent for being in the wrong place at the wrong time." She winks my way. "I guess it's a toss-up at this point who will trip over a corpse first."

"Gee, thanks," I say just as the chime on the door goes off and my own nightmare begins.

CHAPTER 3

*I*n walks a six-foot-tall wall of muscles carrying the most adorable pooch you ever did see, and every woman in the bakery with functioning ovaries stops to gawk his way—and at the handsome detective holding him, too. Have I mentioned the fitted Italian suit the detective is wearing? Cooper is basically a masterpiece in motion.

The little furball in his arms wiggles with excitement and he's as cute as a pumpkin patch. Instantly, the bakery erupts in a chorus of coos, as if someone unleashed a horde of adorable kittens—or in this case, puppies.

"*Watson,*" we all cry at once at the furry little cutie and Lottie runs over and steals the fluffy little floof right out of Cooper Knox's arms.

"Would you look at this little angel?" Lottie sings. "My heart just melted faster than a marshmallow in hot cocoa. I'm claiming this cutie as my own personal Halloween treat."

Watson would be the butter blonde golden shepherd

puppy that Cooper and I inadvertently adopted together about a month ago, and we've been swapping him out between us as any good co-parents would do. Mostly he stays at my place, but when I need to be here, Cooper takes the little guy to work with him.

"What's going on?" Cooper sheds a short-lived smile. With his dark wavy hair and marbled blue-green eyes, my heart or my hormones never stood a chance.

Niki sheds her own quick grin, albeit far more mischievous. "We were just talking about Effie's knack for stumbling into danger. I think we can both agree it's a lot like watching a blind cat in a room full of rocking chairs."

I'd frown at my sister for likening me to a blind cat, but I can't take my eyes off the lethally good-looking detective in front of me.

And why a blind cat? Is that the vibe I'm giving off?

Cooper shoots me a stern look as if agreeing and my stomach cinches on cue.

I can't help it. He gets me with that stern expression each and every time.

Who wants a guy who smiles like a clown all day when you can have Cupertino Lazzari give you dirty looks every chance he gets?

Don't judge me. I've always had a hankering for the dark side.

Suze shrugs as she walks away. "Whether it's Effie tripping over a body or Lottie following the scent of trouble like a bloodhound, I have a feeling Honey Hollow is about to get spookier than a haunted house on Halloween night."

Cooper nods my way. "I have a feeling she's right."

"Why is that?" I practically hop over the counter in an effort to lean his way.

"Because you live here," he flatlines.

"What about me, big boy?" Niki asks while swinging her hips his way like a sultry witch on a broomstick. "Let's not count me out of the fun. I may have the grace of a drunken zombie, but my gut instincts are as sharp as a vampire's fangs. I can get spooky with the best of them."

I can attest to that. She's scared her last three boyfriends right out of town.

The chime goes off on the door once again and in struts Naomi Turner, a sultry seductress with a reputation for turning heads and dragging any man she wants straight to bed.

And if history proves to be the best teacher, then I already know which man she has her sights set on.

She swoops across the room, her eyes laser-focused on Cooper as her lips curve into a seductive smile that could charm the fangs right off a vampire.

"Well, well, well, if it isn't Detective Knox," the stunning brunette purrs, her voice dripping with enough seduction to make any halfway decent saint blush. "It seems you've stumbled upon quite the welcoming committee." She takes a moment to glower my way. "I hope you're not easily frightened," she says, gliding her finger down his tie.

Cooper chuckles. "I can handle a cupcake or two." He glances my way and my insides bisect with heat at the thought of being one of the cupcakes in question. "So how are you doing?" he asks and Naomi lights up like a Christmas tree.

I can't help but frown at him.

Why would he care how she's doing?

Unless he's about to arrest her for a homicide, I don't see any business he has with this woman. We both know she spent all last month trying to sink her claws into him.

"Funny you should ask." Her eyes twinkle his way. "I've got a juicy secret to share. I'll be moonlighting over at the new Tavern of Terror by the lake. I'm helping out as a hostess until they find someone to permanently fill the position."

"The Tavern of Terror?" Lottie asks. "That's a part of that new haunted house attraction just down the street, isn't it?"

"That's right," Naomi says. "A couple of investors decided on profiting from the fact this town is haunted from top to bottom and they're running a haunted house with a restaurant on the ground floor. It's bound to give your mama's haunted bed and breakfast a run for its ghostly money."

Everyone knows Miranda Lemon's bed and breakfast is haunted by genuine ghosts—or so the rumor goes. Seeing that Suze happens to live there doesn't surprise me at all. In fact, it wouldn't surprise me if Suze herself was the reason for the permanent haunting at that place.

Hey? Maybe Suze is a ghost?

Nah. We're not that lucky.

Naomi winks over at Cooper just as Lily slides over a scone and a latte to go for her bestie.

"Anyway, it's going to be the hottest spot in town for some spine-tingling fun," Naomi tells him in an effort to lure him to her zombie-riddled lair. "You should swing by tonight and join the fright fest."

"Actually, I am headed that way this evening," he tells her. "I guess I'll see you there."

Naomi takes off and Niki is the first to growl his way.

"Don't fall for it, Coop," Niki warns. "That temptress is about to suck your soul out by way of your—"

"*Niki*," I hiss and shake my head at her.

"I was about to say toes," she insists. "Should I concerned about some competition?" Niki hikes a brow at him.

"You've got nothing to worry about," he's quick to assure her as Suze glides a coffee and a chocolate glazed cruller his way—Coop's usual. "I'm not falling for her seductive siren song." He casts a quick glance at me. "I've got enough mysteries to unravel when it comes to women."

He's got that right. Although if he unravels mine, it might land us both in the grave. As it stands, he's the only one staring at an open hole in the ground. And I'm the unlucky soul that's been sent to push him in.

"Ooh, and dinner at the Tavern of Terror," Lottie says while nuzzling with that furball who steals half the bed at night—my bed to be exact. "You'll have to tell us what it's like."

"Talk about a coinkydink." Niki grins his way. "Effie and I were plotting a dinner at the Tavern of Terror tonight ourselves. I guess we'll see you there."

Cooper cocks a brow at me. "I guess you will. I'll see you later." He nods as he scoops up Watson and ducks out of the bakery.

And just like that, our impromptu date is locked and loaded and ready to go—or in this case, blow.

The Tavern of Terror.

Just the mention of it sends a shiver down my spine.

Halloween is almost upon us—a night where tricks abound and secrets spill like candy.

Here's hoping my own secrets can stay in place and Cooper is none the wiser to my Glock-wielding ways.

Although that whiteboard behind his desk with a picture of every one of my so-called hits does raise a brow. Cooper was assigned to the task of unraveling the mystery that landed a rash of men in the ER with bullet wounds, and yet not one of them wanted to file an official report. He's already let me know he thinks it's a sloppy mob job.

Sure, those may not have been his exact words, but I know he was thinking it. And sadly, I would be the one doling out the sloppy hits.

Face it, he'll be onto me soon enough. But I'll do everything I can to divert it.

"Buckle up," I say to Niki as Suze and Lily get back to work. "I have a feeling this Halloween is going to be filled with more twists and turns than a haunted corn maze."

"And let's hope those twists don't involve murder," Lottie says as she walks by.

I'd agree, but I don't think we're that lucky.

CHAPTER 4

The Tavern of Terror is located at the foot of Honey Lake, along the strip that houses other restaurants and businesses, in a giant run-down mansion that just so happens to overlook the water. The building is tall and dilapidated and looks as if it's worked hard its whole life to turn into the perfect haunted house for Honey Hollow.

"How do I look?" Niki asks, adjusting her ears and tail. She's donned a black leotard and not much else, with the exception of those pink glittering ears sitting over her head and that whip she's wielding that she's trying to pass off as a tail.

"Like a cat in heat." I adjust my own tail. "How do I look?"

"Like a bunny who showed up at the wrong mansion."

"If Cooper is here, then it's the right one," I say, adjusting the pink ears sitting on top of my head. I, too, have opted for a leotard, white with matching tights, along with a pink tutu and sparkling pink heels that are guaranteed to give me a parting gift—blisters. "The things I do for love," I say, smashing my toes to the edge of the shoes in hopes to stave off the obvious. "Not that I'm in love with him," I quickly correct. "I'm just dressing to impress the man—"

"The man you're destined to bury not marry?" she teases.

"I was going to say the man who is the father of my puppy. And I am not going to bury *or* marry the man."

"You may not be the one burying him, but you'll be the reason someone out there has to."

"I don't want to talk about it," I say as I snarl at the haunted hovel before us. And I'm using the word *hovel* loosely.

Can a mansion qualify as a hovel?

If any oversized house can qualify, it's this one. Spiderwebs and skeletons abound, there's a shadow of a creature with horns that stands fifteen feet tall pressed against the house, and purple and red lights flicker throughout every last window.

The sound of eerie mood music emanates from the speakers and the fog machines surrounding this place are pumping out so much mist it's seeping over half of the lake from what I can see.

The sun has set, and all of the ghouls and boys of this spooky town have dressed to the haunted nines for the night. It doesn't hurt that there's a big sign out front that reads, *wear a costume and get a free cannoli or five dollars off the haunted house attraction!*

I think we all know I'm here for the free cannoli. My life has inadvertently become a haunted house attraction that I can't seem to escape from. And the costume I'm forced to wear day to day clearly didn't come with a thinking cap because if it had, I wouldn't get myself into half the bullet-shaped pickles I'm in.

A spooky dressed crowd passes us by as they head inside, and I pull Niki in close.

"We'd better get in there before they run out of dessert," I tell her.

"They're not running out of nothin'," Niki says. "I stopped by Hairway to Heaven before I got dressed. And while Mom did up my *do*, she gave me the rundown on this place. It turns out, this haunted house is just a gimmick for the grand opening to get the town to try out the new restaurant. Once the calendar turns to November, they'll be hanging a sign with the real name, The Tavern on the Lake. It's an Italian joint owned by two brothers. According to Mom's connections, they're already giving Mangias a run for their money as the best Italian food in town."

"No kidding?" I gasp at the thought.

Mangias is a cute little Italian eatery right across the street from the Cutie Pie Bakery and Cakery. And seeing that Main Street butts right up to the lake, it's just a stone's throw from here.

And let's hope they don't throw any stones. Italians can be a competitive bunch. Let's hope they don't throw any meatballs either.

"Well, Mangias is still my favorite," I say. "I know which side my garlic bread is buttered. Let's get inside and see what they're up against."

We head through the double door entry and the foyer is

black as pitch, save for a candle next to the reception counter. And standing before us just so happens to be the scariest witch I've ever seen—Naomi Turner.

"What are you supposed to be?" she snarls my way. "Cute cat ears, Niki," she seethes without ever taking her eyes off of me.

Figures. Why do mean girls always love Niki?

"Don't mind me," I tell her. "I'm just here to hop right through your worst nightmare." I'd laugh if it wasn't true. The thought of me pumping a bullet into the heart of the man we both seem to be vying for sounds like a nightmare for everyone involved—Cooper included.

"You are my nightmare," she says with a malevolent smile. "Or am I yours? Will you be dining first or walking through the house of horrors in order to work up your appetite?"

"We're cutting right to the chase—free cannolis," Niki says and I can only dream she's right.

Those just so happen to be two of my favorite words, *free* and *cannoli*. Put the two together and you've got a delicious dream come true.

"Dinner for two it is," she says, pulling out a round wooden dish and then promptly taking off her head and placing it onto the platter.

Naomi's head blinks up at us and smiles. "Happy Halloween."

CHAPTER 5

"*AAAGGH!*" Niki and I scream in unison.

But Naomi's headless body is undeterred as she holds her head on a platter—quite literally—and leads us to what looks like a haunted living room until we hit an enormous back patio that overlooks Honey Lake.

The patio is adorned with purple twinkle lights that crisscross overhead like a canopy, along with garlands of fall leaves that look as if they were hosed down with glitter.

A small pumpkin with a candle in it sits nestled on each table, and not only is the place packed, but almost everyone here is wearing a costume. But it's not the guests that garner my attention, it's the glittering purple headstones that are attached to the backs of the chairs that give this place all the appeal of the Honey Hollow Cemetery.

The same spooky music seeps from the speakers, and the mist from those fog machines gives this place the right amount of spooktacular vibes it's looking for.

"Welcome to the graveyard." Naomi giggles from the platter and both Niki and I recoil in horror.

"How are you doing that?" I all but shout at Naomi Turner's head sitting on what looks to be an old wooden lazy Susan.

"Sorry, but I signed an NDA," she sputters. "I'm not allowed to ruin the magic. Seat yourselves, would you? My head is killing me." She saunters back in the direction she came from and both Niki and I shudder.

"Oh, look"—Niki perks up as she cranes her neck to the left—"There's Aunt Cat and Carlotta, and they happen to be seated with about six shirtless ogres."

I glance that way and find my aunt and her good friend Carlotta—a couple of mischief mavens if ever there were some—seated with a handful of green men with enough muscles to bench press all of Vermont if need be.

Niki clucks her tongue. "Good to know this night has enough treats to balance out the tricks. Have fun with Coop." She nods ahead and, sure enough, Cooper is here and he's got a seat right on the water. And by his side is the cutest little furry sidekick you ever did see. "I'm headed to greener pastures." She starts to take off then backtracks. "And don't you dare pull the trigger without me. It's not fair you get to have all the fun."

I take a moment to glower at her. "You'd better learn to whisper or I'll be pulling a trigger, all right."

She takes off with a whoop and I make a beeline to my mark.

"Is this seat taken or is it reserved for Naomi Turner's head on a platter?"

Coop ticks his head to the side and looks slightly dazed

by the thought. "I don't know. According to the gravestone attached to that seat, Naomi Turner died six weeks ago under suspicious circumstances. It says she had her head severed in a kitchen accident."

"Oh, come on," I say, landing across from him. "You know we're not that lucky."

We share a quick laugh and I note how handsome he looks with his dark suit and dark hair combed back, still dewy from the shower. His woodsy cologne permeates the area, and those blue eyes of his shine under the purple twinkle lights like a pair of magical moonbeams.

Watson jumps and barks until I give him a full-body rub down.

"Great news," Cooper says, sliding a menu my way. "This place serves Italian. I have a feeling it's going to be one of our favorites."

My stomach squeezes tight when he says the word *our*.

A headless waitress comes by and we quickly put in our orders as follows: appetizers—antipasto salami and cheese trio, main course—chicken cacciatore for me, beef braciola for him, half a pan of lasagna to split, and a side of meat-balls with gravy, aka the house marinara.

Both Coop and I know it would be impossible to judge this place appropriately without a lasagna and meatballs to juxtapose against the ones they serve at Mangias.

No sooner does the waitress and her rogue head stroll off than a woman crops up with long dark hair, red glossy lips filled like helium balloons, and a body that belongs to Jessica Rabbit.

She's got a pricey handbag dangling from her shoulder and is wearing enough bling to signal to the space station.

She's donned a red sequin dress that clings to her like melted wax, along with a pair of horns sitting on her head and a red pointy tail that she's holding like a leash.

By her side is a man in a zoot suit with a fedora dipped over his forehead. He has dark hair, dark eyes, and judging by that wicked smile curving on his lips, a wicked soul to match.

"Well, look who the cat dragged in." She honks out a laugh while looking at Cooper. "Or should I say dirty rabbit?"

Hey? I'm not dirty. But talk to me after dinner when this white leotard looks as if it took part in a massacre. I'd feel guilty about it, but it is October, and red sauce looks a lot like blood. It's a timely fashion choice on my part.

"Loretta?" Cooper rises out of his seat and pulls the woman with the forked tongue in for a quick embrace.

It would figure he knows her. Cooper is a looker—and he seems to attract a bunch of oddballs because of it. Case in point, Naomi Turner.

The woman honks out another laugh and sounds like a dying seal.

Speaking of the oddballs he attracts, I'm guessing the naughty devil has had her due—or her way with the good detective.

Although she doesn't seem Cooper's type with that designer handbag that costs more than my car, the fact she's dripping with diamonds, and those eyelashes that nearly touch the twinkle lights.

If they ever were together, it was just a fling. Judging by the fact she looks as if she looted a jewelry store, he couldn't afford to keep her. Not on his salary anyway. And if it were true love, he'd be robbing banks by now.

She looks my way and laughs. "So who's the whore with the chore of being your plus-one for the night?"

I straighten.

Watson growls.

Did she just say *whore with the chore?* My mouth falls open because I think I just discovered someone far more vulgar than my sister—and perhaps any other woman outside of Loretta's homeland of Hell.

CHAPTER 6

"*I*gnore her," Cooper says, landing back in his seat right here at the Tavern of Terror as the devil herself regales us with her presence. "Effie, this is my sister, Loretta Solemina Lazzari. Loretta, this is Effie. We're new," he tells her sternly. "Be nice."

We're new?

I practically mouth the words.

How has Cooper Knox, aka Cupertino Lazzari, suddenly come around to the dark side and want to claim me as his own?

Is he onto me? Does he know I have a hit out against him?

Hey! Maybe that makes him like me more? Men are funny like that.

"So you're the new squeeze." Loretta's eyes slit to nothing. "Just know I don't take too kindly to anyone messing with my big bro. I'll be watching you." She points to her eyes then mine with the threat before perking up again. "Coop, I want you to meet my friend Sal the Sausage

Marino. He's my bestie's hubby." She steps aside and reveals the dark-haired man in a zoot suit with the fedora as she winks his way. "Sal and his brother Johnny just opened up this place. *Yo, Johnny.*" She shoves her fingers in her mouth and whistles loud enough to wake the dead and, sure enough, everyone seated in this makeshift cemetery is suddenly at attention.

Another zoot suit-wearing Italian looker struts this way, same dark hair, same eyes, and I'm betting same sooted soul as Sal the Sausage.

"This is my main squeeze, Johnny the Meatball Marino," Loretta proudly states. "And he's the only Marino that counts." She does her impression of a honking seal once again while giving both brothers a pinch on the cheek. "If your food isn't to your liking, blame this one." She hitches her head toward the Sausage. "On the other hand, Johnny can do no wrong. Now if you'll excuse us, we've got guests to greet." She swings her pointy tail like a pendulum as the three of them drift off to haunt the next table.

"So you've got a sister," I say.

Who happens to be about as charming as my own. Or at least the sister I showed up with.

"I've got three," he says with a depleted smile. "And two brothers to boot."

"There's six of you? And I thought we were a big family with five," I say and Watson barks and jumps. "And you showed up with an entire litter." I laugh as I give him a scratch.

"Speaking of litters." Cooper leans on his elbows. "How big of a family are you looking to build?"

Is he talking *children*?

"You have a lot of positive attributes," he says without so much as a smile. "You're smart. You have a talent with baked goods. And you seem to have a talent with people, too. To know you is to love you. I bet you're going to be a great mom someday."

I nearly fall over just as a headless waitress arrives with a trio of hard cheeses and a trio of salami to kick our night off in the right direction. If only Cooper wasn't walking around with a target on his back, he would have already kicked it off in the right direction.

I'm not sure what's gotten into him tonight, but he's hitting all the notes that a girl like me wants to hear. Too bad the only song I'll be singing has all but one note—to the tune of my Glock.

I frown at the thought. Although admittedly, it's not enough to make me lose my appetite.

Set before us is a tray of Parmigiano Reggiano, Pecorino Romano, and Grana Padano cheeses, and each one is flaky, chunkier, saltier, and tastier than the last. Each sits behind a tiny little label as does the meat trio with their delicate slices curled into perfect little meaty roses— Genoa, spicy soppressata, and Italian dry salami.

We dive into the platter—the only headless platter around, mind you—and we both moan with approval.

"All right, Effie." He nods my way, his lips curled a touch, and I think he's actually bedroom eyeing me. "What's your favorite?"

A small sigh escapes me. Is there a more perfect man on the planet than the one who longs to hear my thoughts on hard cheeses? And salted meats, too, of course.

"It's a three-way tie for the cheese," I say. "But as far as the deli snacks, this is basically your *Sofie's Choice* of salami. You're not going to lose any which way, but if I had to rank them, I'd say my number one pick is the Italian dry. It has the exact tang I'm looking for when I think about a good salami. Soppressata and Genoa are tied for second. Genoa is great for those white bread and mayo sandwiches, the sandwiches of my youth. As for the soppressata, I'd like to put that on my next pizza, along with pepperoni. And once in a while, I've been known to make a sandwich out of soppressata and pepperoni when I'm feeling extra cheeky."

Cooper gives a slight applause. "I couldn't have said it better myself."

Watson gives a chirp of a bark and dances on his hind legs, just begging to get in on the action so I toss him a salty rose.

The sounds of ear-piercing screams come from the haunted house behind us and everyone on the patio turns to look that way.

"Sounds as if Naomi is losing her head again," I say.

"Maybe so." He frowns as his left elbow pats his waist to ensure his weapon is in place. "But I'd better go check it out. Don't eat my meatball." He winks my way. "Come on, Watson." He picks up the leash. "Let's check this out."

Don't eat his meatball?

And that wink?

Dies.

How is this turning out to be the perfect night?

The sound of voices quarreling garners my attention and I look up to see Sal the Sausage having it out over by the side gate with a man about his age, same dark hair, extra bushy brows. He looks familiar to me, but with those purple lights washing him out, I couldn't tell my father from an alien at this point.

The bushy-browed man shoves Sal in the chest before darting out the gate. And soon, Loretta takes his place, swatting Sal's chest and shouting the word *cheater* for all to hear. Or at least all that are eavesdropping, which would be me.

Cheater?

Hey, didn't she mention he was married to her bestie? I'd run if I were him.

On second thought, I hope he stands still. I'd like to throw my meatball at him. That is, if I had it to throw.

Another few minutes drift by and soon our main entrées arrive.

The food is going to get cold.

Maybe I should text Cooper.

I'm about to do just that when a tiny butter-colored furball whizzes right past me and right out the side gate.

"*Watson,*" I cry, glancing back, but there's no sign of Cooper. "Oh, for Frankenstein's sake," I growl. If I don't get him, he might end up a permanent fixture of this haunted house—as a ghost.

Doesn't the perky pooch know the mean streets of Honey Hollow are no place for a cutie pie like him?

I abandon my meal—not an easy thing to do—and ditch out the side gate and promptly fall over a soft lump of— a man?

"*Gah!*" I jump to my feet and scoop up Watson in one herculean move.

Lying sprawled out beneath me is a man in a dark zoot suit with a fedora partially covering his face.

"*Effie*," Cooper calls out as he runs out the gate right after me, and in his arms is—Watson?

"What the—?" I gag without finishing my thought.

"Who's this?" Cooper asks as he looks down at the body, undeterred by the fact that our cute pooch just multiplied before our very eyes. Honestly, I much prefer it to losing his furry little head.

"It's probably just a prop for this house of horrors," I say, giving the makeshift corpse a kick in the nuts.

Cooper kneels down and rolls the guy onto his back and I gasp at the fact there's not one but two bullet holes putzing up his nice white dress shirt—and perhaps his life. His hat falls off and I clearly recognize his face.

Coop checks for a pulse before shaking his head at me.

Sal the Sausage is dead.

CHAPTER 7

"He's dead?" I practically shout the words as Cooper quickly calls it into the station, and within seconds, the sound of sirens does its best to eclipse the creepy music and intermittent screams here at the Tavern of Terror.

The house of horrors behind us is flooded with bodies, and now we've got one in the alleyway, too— a dead one.

My heart thumps like a jackhammer as I take in the scene. Lights flicker and shadows elongate as the spooky music fills the air. It feels as if I've just stepped into a horror flick, and I have a feeling I'm playing a starring role.

Sal the Sausage lies splayed out. His face an eerie shade of blue and his white dress shirt is punctuated with two bright red dots where the bullets took him out. Whoever did this was either a good shot or was close enough to reach out and touch him—with their *gun*.

"I can't believe this," I mutter as my heart thumps like a jackhammer.

"Somehow I believe it," Cooper says, handing Watson to

me, and now my arms are filled with two wiggling puppies —who, by the way, look identical. "It's like you're a calling card, Effie."

"A calling card for what?"

"The Grim Reaper."

"You know what they say." I cringe at the thought. "'Tis the season."

He shoots me a stern look.

I lift my shoulders to my ears. "Too soon?"

Within moments, the area is swarmed with officers and soon they're cordoning the area off with bright yellow caution tape.

I spot Niki, my Aunt Cat, and Carlotta headed this way.

Great. Just what I need.

The three of them gasp as they spot the body.

"What have you gotten yourself into now?" Niki shrieks, and if I'm not mistaken, there's a hint of delight in her voice. She's wicked that way.

"Don't look at me. I was just chasing this one"—I say, nodding to the Watson look-alike in my arms—"when a corpse decided to crash the party."

Technically, the corpse got here first, but the three women before me have never been so hot on accurate details. They're more interested in gossip and making a ruckus. Come to think of it, they're experts at both.

"Sounds to me like someone is working on an alibi." Aunt Cat squints at me with suspicion. Her dark hair is teased to high heaven and she's dressed in some sort of Roaring Twenties' outfit—a short beaded frock with lots of long pearl necklaces and a feather sticking out of her head. "Are you sure this wasn't one of Jimmy's assignments?"

I frown at the woman for daring to go there, and with a cast of thousands around no less.

"No," I say. "For all I know, it might be a Halloween prank gone wrong."

Carlotta grunts as she inspects the corpse, "Remind me to never invite you to a dinner party." She shrugs. She happens to have that same Roaring Twenties' vibe happening but with darker back alley intentions written all over her. Come to think of it, that's sort of her MO in general when it comes to life. "But then, I don't throw dinner parties so we're good there." She takes a moment to give me the stink eye. "I think my Lot Lot's luck might be rubbing off on you."

Lot Lot would be my boss, Lottie, who happens to be Carlotta's biological child. Carlotta left Lottie at a fire station when she was an infant, and luckily Lottie was raised by a decent family, the Lemons.

But Carlotta is back in town and she and Lottie share the same caramel wavy locks, more gray than caramel for Carlotta. In fact, Carlotta looks exactly like my beautiful boss with the exception that someone hit the fast-forward button and aged her about fifty years.

"Lottie has nothing to do with my rotten luck," I grunt. "I've been walking around like a broken mirror for a lot longer than I've known just about anyone." Not a fact I'm particularly proud of but true, nonetheless.

The pooches in my arms wiggle and dance and Niki quickly takes Watson's look-alike from me while I let Watson down and wrap his leash around my wrist so he can't accidentally lead the way to another body. Not that it was him who did it in the first place. But I'm sort of a lightning-strikes-twice kind of a gal and I'd hate to tempt fate *twice* in one night.

"Who the heck is this little furry cutie?" Niki asks while the ball of blond fur licks her face silly.

"No idea. There's no tag on him. I just found him out here," I say. "Why don't you go try to turn him in to the lost and found or something? I'll stick around and look for clues."

"You mean for the killer?" Aunt Cat clasps at her throat, and yet she, too, has a look of unmitigated glee in her eyes. I'd say it's contagious, but the fact is, all three of these women are more than slightly deranged.

Okay, so I fit the bill, too.

What can I say? We like to dole out justice with the best of them.

"No, I want to look for the owner," I say. "But for the killer, too."

I *so* meant the killer.

Niki takes off and the three of us do our best to scour the area as we split ways.

A crowd has gathered so there's not a lot of room to hunt and peck. I'm about to give up when I see something just shy of the caution tape that catches my eye. It's a trail of red sequins that glitters just past the gate and out into the street.

I quickly take a few pictures of it.

"What are you doing?" a deep voice resonates from behind and I jump just as Cooper squints in the direction that my phone is pointed.

"I, uh…" I grimace because he's not going to like what I'm about to say. "Look at that." I point right at the menacing crimson trail. "The red stuff." I nod his way, waiting for him to do the DNA math.

He steps over and picks one up by way of the tip of his finger. "It's not blood. It's just a piece of some silly costume."

"I know it's not blood, it's red sequins." I nod expectantly, but still he's giving me nothing.

Watson wiggles and barks up at him as if saying, *come on, you're supposed to be the detective around here.*

"Who was wearing red sequins tonight?" I wave my hand back at the patio, but that look of confusion on his face only continues to grow. "*Salmonella.*"

"What?" He inches back as if I've just accosted him with my words.

"Your sister, Salmonella."

"You mean Loretta Solemina." He frowns. "Okay, so it's hers. She's been in and out of this place all night. It's her boyfriend's deal. And if you'll learn anything about my sister, it's that she likes to take over. Speaking of which, would you mind taking Watson home tonight? I won't be heading to my place any time soon."

"No problem," I say and he leans in and lands a kiss to my cheek.

"Thank you." His eyes stay hooked to mine a moment too long and I bite down on a smile because, holy moly, the detective has turned up the charm like nobody's business this evening.

He steps away and that goofy grin glides right off my face.

I'll admit, his sudden uptick in interest does make me wonder.

"What do you think?" I ask, scooping Watson up. "Am I irresistible or am I irresistible?"

Before Watson can so much as give me a bark of approval, Niki comes back and hands me the look-alike pooch.

"No dice," she says. "Nobody knows who he belongs to. Tag, you're it. I don't do dogs. But I'm open to ogres and I've got a hot one on the hook. Naomi says she'll put up some posters. We'll talk in the morning. Try not to kill anyone while I'm gone. Try not to hog all the fun." She takes off, presumably to have a little fun herself—seeing that she suddenly has a hankering for not-so-little green men.

Aunt Cat and Carlotta come back looking dismayed.

"We've got nothing," Aunt Cat says.

"That's right," Carlotta snips. "Just another dead end. Get it? *Dead end?*"

"Stop," I tell her as the pup in my arms wiggles and licks my face. "I've got a killer to track down."

I crane my neck toward the crowd, on the hunt for a certain female Lazzari. After all, I did see her arguing with the deceased just minutes before I found the body. And if I know anything about the Lazzaris, they're prone to spicy tempers and are not above popping off a few shots as a way to end an argument.

"Forget the killer," Carlotta says, giving the pooch in my arms a scratch. "I need to find me a man who licks like this."

"I'd take one half as excited to see me," Aunt Cat grunts.

"Cheer up," Carlotta says, bumping her hip to her bestie. "I know a man who will be twice as excited to see

39

us. The pizza delivery guy. Let's head to my place and try to beat him there. We can play a hand of poker. I'm in need of some quick cash and I know you're good for it."

"That's because you cheat," Aunt Cat says as the two of them take off.

I glance back at the body on the ground as the coroner's office shows up and begins to photograph the scene for themselves.

My Aunt Cat isn't the only cheat around here—Loretta accused Sal the Sausage of the very same thing.

Someone out there killed a man in cold blood tonight.

My eyes stray back to that trail of red sequins that leads straight to the body.

And I wonder if I've already cracked the case.

CHAPTER 8

The next morning I saunter into the bakery where the smell of freshly baked goodies swirls around me like a warm hug.

It's my day off, but after the whirlwind of last night, I need a little pick-me-up to process everything. And what better way to do that than with a few dozen crullers? Okay, so I'll go easy and stick to just one—dozen.

Since no one claimed Watson's doppelgänger, the fuzzy little tot spent the night at my place. And instead of sleeping, these two cute clowns decided the night would be better spent chasing one another's tails and chewing up the trashy romance novels right off my bookshelf. Now I'm not only down a good night's sleep, but I have no indecent reading material to land me in La-La Land.

I find a seat near the giant smiling pumpkin taped to the window. And within seconds, Lily greets me with a chocolate cupcake with a mountain of icing molded on top of it to make it look like a pretty pink brain.

"Special spooky delivery for our resident sleuth." She

wrinkles her nose as she leans in. "Thanks for finding the body. I won the office pool between you and Lottie."

"I aim to please," I grunt, pulling the cupcake closer. "Brains for breakfast? Now that's what I call starting the day off right." At this point, I could use all the brains I can get.

I take a moment to admire the intricate details that make it look almost too real to eat.

Almost.

Let's not get carried away. A sugar infusion is a sugar infusion. I'm pretty much a the-more-the-merrier type of girl when it comes to sweet treats.

But my attention is quickly diverted as a chorus of barks starts up as both Watson and his look-alike bounce around at my feet.

And upon hearing those barks, Lottie and Suze hightail it this way posthaste.

"Oh my word!" Lottie quickly scoops up Watson's twin. "Did our little cutie reproduce overnight?"

"He's not that talented yet," I say. "We picked this guy up at the Tavern of Terror last night. With all the melee, I think he got separated from his owner. I left my number with Naomi, and she's making posters, but so far no one has stepped up to claim him." I pause for a moment. "By the way, did you know that Naomi Turner's head functions as a removable device?"

Lottie thumps out a laugh. "Her twin might be my bestie, but I'd swear that Naomi has been running around with her head chopped off for years. What's this cutie pie's name?"

"He doesn't have one," I say. "Or at least not that I know

of. We should probably give him one for the time being."

"Ooh, I've always wanted to name a dog," Lily says, scratching the pup behind the ears.

"I've got one," Suze says. "*Sherlock*. You know, to go with Watson."

I shake my head. "As much as I love the idea, I don't want Watson to feel like he's second best. Everyone knows Sherlock steals the spotlight."

"Okay then." Suze squints at the puppy and it looks as if she's silently casting a pox on the poor pooch. And knowing Suze, she might be. "How about Trouble? Seems fitting, considering the fact he's a man."

Lily chuckles. "Or Chase, because, let's face it, men are about as predictable as a dog chasing its own tail."

"*Eh*." Suze shrugs. "Or we can call him Drooly. Always loyal, always drooling, just like the men Lottie attracts."

Suze should know. One of the men Lottie has attracted is Suze's son, Noah. And I've witnessed his lovesick ways more than a few times when it comes to my boss. The man really does drool.

I shake my head at the thought. "Maybe we shouldn't insult our furry friends by comparing them to the male species."

Suze snorts. "Oh, come on, Effie. You know as well as I do that men are just like dogs. They bark, they beg, and at the end of the day, they're all chasing after the same hour-glass-shaped bone."

Lottie laughs as if she knows it's true. And she should since it's mostly true in her case.

"How about Chip?" Lottie offers. "You know, like a chip off the old block?"

"I don't know. I'd be hard-pressed not to believe they weren't related, but Watson isn't his father."

"True," Lottie says. "But it sure is spooky how much they look alike."

"*Spooky!*" I practically shout. "That's a perfect name. And not only that, but I think I'll call the breeder I got Watson from and see if she's missing a puppy. I bet that's a spooky feeling."

"Spooky it is," Lily declares just as a mob floods the bakery. "Welcome to the family, little guy. Come on, Suze. Let's hit the registers before we have a cupcake revolt on our hands. And don't worry, Effie. As soon as the crowd dies down, I'll sling a plate of crullers your way."

"You know my love language," I say as they take off.

Lottie falls into the seat across from me and leans in. "All right, spill it, Effie," she says, giving little Spooky a hearty scratch. "Noah says there was a homicide at the Tavern of Terror last night and that you found the body! What exactly went down last night?"

Noah as in Homicide Detective Noah Fox. He's one of Cooper's co-workers.

I sigh as I spin the delicious-looking brain set in front of me. "I'm not sure what happened. The whole night was off—from Naomi's removable primal apex to the fact Cooper was saying all the things I've been wanting to hear."

"*Ooh.*" She wiggles her shoulders as she says it. "I'm glad that's finally headed in the right direction."

"I am, too." I frown at the thought. "And even though he seemed sincere, the night was almost too perfect. Anyway, the universe squashed that like a bug pretty quickly. I met

Cooper's sister, a real character who called me a less-than-savory name. She's the one who introduced us to Sal the Sausage. Then shortly after that, we heard screams. Cooper went to see if there was something nefarious happening, outside of the fact we were dining in a haunted house. And that's when I saw that little guy." I nod to Spooky. "I thought Watson was trying to make a getaway, so I chased after him and nearly tripped right over Sal the Sausage. Cooper was on my heels and he's the one that confirmed Sal was dead."

Lottie cringes. "I'm sorry. I know how it feels to stumble upon a body."

I'll say she does. I think she's found close to two dozen —or three.

And I hear the coroner buys body bags in bulk because of it.

"So did you see anything suspicious?" she asks. "Noah says someone shot the guy in close range. The killer could have left behind a clue or two."

I'm about to fill her in on that trail of shiny red sequins that led right to the parking lot, but a customer drops a box of cookies and soon screaming and barking ensue.

She lands Spooky into my lap and takes off to deal with the cookie chaos just as two frazzled-looking battle-axes head this way. And I mean that in the nicest way possible.

Mostly.

Aunt Cat and Carlotta are clad in terry cloth workout gear, fuchsia for Aunt Cat and orange for Carlotta. Their faces glow a shade of hot pink and they both sport sweatbands across their foreheads. And it's as disconcerting of a sight as one might think.

"Looking for a porthole to the eighties?" I ask.

"More like a porthole into murder," Aunt Cat says, handing a simple white envelope my way and my heart sinks to my feet. "We just got back from Leeds."

I'd ask if they ran all the way, but my vocal cords don't seem to work at the moment.

That seemingly innocent envelope is Uncle Jimmy's way of giving me instructions as to who falls next in line on my kill list.

The funny thing is, my last assignment is still running around with breath in his lungs. And if I were Cooper, I'd add that to the roster of my positive attributes—*allows me to live another day.*

"It's a bit soon for this, don't you think?" I gulp hard, trying to juggle the puppies and the envelope.

Personally, I'm hoping one of these fluffy floofs will gobble it down so I can finally use the excuse, *the dog ate my homework.*

Aunt Cat shrugs. "If Jimmy wants someone out there wiped off the planet, it's never soon enough."

"Go on," Carlotta says with her eyes agog as if she can hardly stand the suspense. "You never know whose name you're going to see on the inside of one of those business cards from the Grim Reaper. It could be the sheriff, another certain homicide detective, a sexy-looking judge, a manipulative mayor, or even me."

I make a face at her. She just listed both men who are vying for Lottie's heart, along with the mayor who happens to be Carlotta's own plus-one. And, of course, she threw herself in there for good measure.

"I promise it's not you," I say, pulling the contents out of the envelope. The others I'm not too sure about.

"You never know," Carlotta says, swiping a finger through the sugary brain before me. "Jimmy and I were hot and heavy once. And I dated his nemesis, Luke Lazzari, too. I wouldn't be surprised if I got caught in the crosshairs of a turf war."

I unfurl the piece of paper and see a name that sends a chill down my spine.

I flash it at Aunt Cat and Carlotta and they both recoil in horror as well.

"Johnny the Meatball Marino," I hiss lower than a whisper. "That's the dead guy's brother. We can't do that to his mama. Clearly, Uncle Jimmy has no idea what transpired last night."

Aunt Cat grimaces at the thought. "Actually, I told him that just as he was handing the envelope my way."

"Well, what did he say?" I ask, unable to take my next breath.

"He said that should make this next hit one for the record books. And then he told me to pass along two little words—*have fun.*"

"Have fun," I growl and both Watson and Spooky growl along with me.

If I didn't know it before, I'm well aware of it now. Uncle Jimmy doesn't have a beating heart. And soon enough, Johnny the Meatball Marino won't either.

Here's to having fun.

I shove the cupcake straight into my mouth, brains and all.

It's time to let the good times roll—all the way to the morgue.

CHAPTER 9

$\mathcal{I}$ left the bakery feeling down and dejected over the fact my next hit is about as bad as my last.

As much as I don't want to pump my shiny new boyfriend full of bullets, I'm less eager to pump them into Johnny the Meatball Marino.

His poor family has been through enough, considering the fact Johnny's brother Sal isn't even cold yet. But the investigation into his murder is growing just that by the minute. Which is why I packed up my pooches and headed back to the scene of the crime. Not only am I on the hunt for clues, but I'd be darned if I let another day slip by without getting my hands on those cannolis. Sure, they won't be free, considering I'm not in costume, but I bet they'll be worth every dollar.

I gasp as I spot the bunny ears sitting on the passenger side of my car and promptly plop them back on my head where those pink fuzzy cuties belong.

It looks as if I'm back in business.

I leash up both Watson and Spooky and we make our

way toward the haunted mansion where everything unraveled for Sal last night.

"Would you wait?" a female voice squawks and I turn around to see Niki barreling this way, her cat ears and that long furry tail adhered to her body. "I've been following you all the way down Main Street. You drive like you're in the Daytona 500. Were you trying to lose me?"

"Lose you? It's a straight line from the bakery to here."

"Well, I wasn't at the bakery," she says, adjusting her ears and taking Spooky's leash from me. "I was at my place of employment, the Honey Pot Diner. Keelie said I could have the rest of the afternoon off."

Keelie would be the manager of the Honey Pot Diner and she also happens to be Naomi Turner's twin sister—the prettier, nicer twin in my opinion. The one who knows how to keep her head about her. As for the Honey Pot Diner, it's attached to the bakery via a walkthrough, so it takes the exact same straight line to get here. But this is Niki I'm dealing with, so it's a moot point.

"Are you ready to get our cannolis on?" I tease as we turn to the dilapidated haunted house covered in enough spiderwebs to blanket the planet twice.

"That and watch you take down the other goof that owns this place. Aunt Cat filled me in on the dirty deets once you sped out the door."

"Nice to know she can keep a secret," I muse as we head on into the dark maw waiting to swallow us whole.

Creepy organ music plays a touch too loud. Naomi Turner greets us, and yet again we watch as she plucks off her noggin, sets it on a platter, and asks us to follow her to the patio.

"Does it ever get old?" I ask her as she leads us through the darkened hallway of horrors with pictures that shift to sinister versions of themselves as we walk past them and a couple of skeletons that look as if they're making out on a dusty sofa nearby.

"Watching people cry out in terror never gets old," that head of hers shouts while doing its best to look up at me. "I rather enjoy watching people look as if they're about to be sick. Sort of the way you look now."

"Don't worry," I tell her. "It's nothing a couple of cannolis can't fix. Although I'm not sure they'll do much for you."

We no sooner get out to the makeshift cemetery that's taken over the back patio than I spot the exact person I was hoping to see, Cooper's sister. She's seated alone, clad in black yoga gear while solemnly staring out at the water.

The sky is growing increasingly dark, the air is nippy and crisp, and those lavender twinkle lights that crisscross overhead cast an unearthly glow over her.

"That's Loretta Salami" I hiss to Niki. "I want to have a word with her."

"You mean Loretta the Black Widow Lazzari," Naomi croaks from the platter. "It's a nickname she's earned, considering she lost two husbands within a couple of years. Her boyfriend, Johnny, is the one that owns this place. If I were him, I'd watch my back for stray bullets."

Niki nudges me. "Or not-so-stray bullets."

Seeing that I'm shooting them, they'll most likely be stray.

"Thanks for the heads-up," I say to Naomi and cringe as we part ways.

Niki and I head straight over to the Black Widow's table and take a seat across from her.

"Loretta," I say as she looks abruptly our way. Her face is powder white, her eyes are heavily outlined with kohl, and her lashes are as thick as a moth's wing and twice as long. Her lips are ruby red, and judging by the dirty look she's giving us, she wishes we were dead. "It's me, *Effie*. We met last night. I just saw you sitting here and wanted to see how you were doing."

"Who?" She reaches for her phone as if she's about to call the cops.

"Cooper's girlfriend," I say. "You know, *the whore with the chore*."

Niki gasps and giggles herself into a conniption and I give her the side-eye before casting the same dirty look to Loretta for making me go there to begin with.

I told Niki all about it late last night when she stopped by with cookies. We may not live together, but since she's always at my place I think it's time to start charging her half the rent.

"Oh yeah." Loretta honks out a laugh like a seal, and the sound alone seems to arrest all activity on the lake. "Where's my big brother?" She cranes her neck past me with a glimmer of hope. "He didn't say anything about bringing his puttana."

Niki chirps out a laugh. "She just called you a whore in two languages."

"I'm aware," I grunt before sitting straight as a pin. "You mean you're meeting Cooper for lunch?"

"Why else would I be sitting alone in a restaurant

without food or drink?" She looks at me like I'm an idiot and I'm starting to feel that way.

It's time to make an exit—and fast.

"Well, it was nice seeing—"

A shadow darkens our table before I can finish my sentence, and considering the fact the sky is almost black as pitch that's saying a lot.

"Well, well." Niki looks up and grins. "Look who the headless puttana dragged in."

CHAPTER 10

$\mathcal{I}$ glance up and, sure enough, I see Detective Cooper Knox frowning at me right here in the middle of a makeshift graveyard out on the patio of the Tavern of Terror.

Coop looks lean and mean in a dark inky suit. His facial scruff and slicked-back hair are on point, and just about every ovary in the vicinity has been put on notice. Especially mine.

Both Watson and Spooky perk up at the sight of him and he quickly offers them both the scratches and pats they're looking for.

"Ladies." Cooper nods to the three of us.

"We were just leaving," I say, jumping out of my seat and he motions for me to sit back down.

"Please stay," he says. "Lunch is on me. It's my treat."

"Hear that?" Niki elbows me in the ribs and nearly takes a lung out. "We don't have to stock up on cannolis. We're getting a free lasagna out of it, too."

"Good thing," I say, giving Cooper a look. "We never did get around to diving into it last night."

"We should get extra," he says with a nod. "We can take the rest home and finish it for dinner."

"Your place or mine?" Niki is quick to accept his offer.

"*Mine.*" I swat her. And I'm nearly tempted to swat Cooper as well, but he's clear across the table next to his name-calling sister.

Why is he suddenly so gung-ho with our relationship? It's as if we've gone from zero to hero in just one night. Although we did share a rather steamy smooch a couple of weeks back.

Hey? I bet he wants a repeat and figures he'd better butter me up to get it. Cooper's no fool, but apparently I am for not realizing it sooner.

The waitress comes by and we put in an order that could double as a catering menu for a football team.

"I'm glad you brought your appetites, ladies." He gives a malevolent smile, and I'm not sure what's going on, but something is definitely percolating under the surface of those baby blues of his.

However, one mystery at a time.

I clear my throat as I shed a forlorn smile in Loretta's direction.

"I'm sorry about your loss," I tell her and, sure enough, Cooper's eyes widen a notch in my direction.

It's clear he's just now realizing that my visit to the Tavern of Terror had very little to do with cannolis—but *not entirely* nothing to do with them. I still plan on inhaling a platter of them and I don't care if they happen to be surrounding Naomi Turner's head.

Come to think of it, I might enjoy them better that way.

"Yeah." Loretta glowers out at the water. "It seems Sal's luck ran out just like his sausages." She shrugs my way. "I do the orders around here. In fact, it was my idea that he and his brother buy this place. It was my idea to have the haunted house and the free cannolis for those in costume." She points from me to Niki. "Silly ears don't count. Anyway, this is my brainchild *and* my baby, and Sal had to go and muck everything up." She's back to glowering at the water.

Cooper lifts a brow my way then to his sister. "Loretta, what's going on? What do you mean muck everything up?"

She turns his way with wild eyes. "What are you, a *stuggot*?" That would be Italian for idiot. "Is this skank eating your brain cells for breakfast?" she barks right at him.

I wouldn't be too offended if I were him. Sometimes we Italians can get a little loud. My mother likes to say that yelling is her love language.

She sure loved us kids a lot growing up.

"Sal is *dead*," Loretta thunders. "Morella is a mess. Johnny is a wreck. He's at the funeral home with the rest of the family making arrangements. They're already going through heck and it hasn't even been twenty-four hours. I'm taking over this place until Johnny gets back on his feet."

"So who's Morella?" I ask and elicit a frown from Cooper.

What? She practically offered up the information.

"I'm so sorry about everything," Cooper says as he wraps an arm around his sister. "What can I do to make things better? You want me to hire someone to take over this place while you catch your breath?"

"*Aww*," both Niki and I coo in unison. He really is a treasure.

He shoots us a look just as the food lands on the table.

Cooper says grace and impresses the heck out of us, and most likely the Big Guy Upstairs, too.

"I'm fine." Loretta shakes off her grief as best she can just as we all dig in. "And to answer your question"—she stabs a knife in my direction with nothing short of a threat —"Morella is Sal's widow. She's also my best friend in the whole wide world. I'd do anything for her, including kill." Her shoulders jump for a second. "Of course, I didn't kill Sal," she's quick to tell her big brother. "But whoever did this is still out there. And you better believe I expect you to lock them up and throw away the key forever." She winks his way and Niki and I exchange a look.

I'll bet dollars to cannolis that Loretta is pulling the wool over her brother's eyes. And knowing how highly Cooper regards his black widow of a baby sister, he'd gladly let her get away with murder.

And I bet that's exactly what Loretta is banking on.

But I forget all about Loretta and her murderous ways as soon as I sink my teeth into that lasagna.

"*Holy wow*," I moan through a bite. "This has got to be the best lasagna I've ever tasted. I quickly shoot Niki a look. "Don't you dare tell our mother."

She shrugs. "Deal. But it'll cost you a cannoli. I might be bursting at the seams once I polish off this masterpiece, but there's always room for dessert—mine and yours."

I growl her way and the dogs join in the growling choir.

"Oh hey." I look over at Cooper. "Watson's look-alike may not have an owner, but we gave him a name. It's Spooky."

"*Aww*, go on and tell him," Niki says. "The man inspects dead bodies for a living. I doubt you'll be able to scare him."

I cast yet another side glance her way. "It's *Spooky*. That's his name."

Loretta grunts, "Come here, you little love bug." She picks up Watson and he proceeds to make a lunge for her lasagna. "Is the mean old lady calling you names?"

Who is she calling a mean old lady?

"You're not so spooky," she coos right at him and he licks her silly. "That's right. *She's* spooky."

"He's not spooky and neither am I," I'm quick to tell her and shoot a dirty look at Cooper for not coming to my spooky defense. Things are about to get spooky, all right. "That's the wrong dog."

"*Oh.*" Loretta tosses Watson to the ground and scoops up Spooky, who does look rather spooked to be in Loretta's arms. Can't say I blame him. He saw the way she dropped his brother like he was a sack of potatoes.

That's it. She's crawled along my last nerve.

"So if you didn't kill Sal, who did?" I get right to the point and freeze because in no way did I mean to say that out loud. Not in front of Cooper anyway.

I plunge a heaping bite of lasagna into my mouth to keep from saying anything else I might quasi-regret.

Loretta shoots daggers my way with her eyes reduced to slits. "I don't know nothin' about nothin'. If you want to know about Sal, you should probably ask his brother." She turns to Cooper. "I'm innocent in all this. You got that?"

She points a glossy red fingernail right at him. "Get this straight. Someone else is going to pay for this." She jumps out of her seat and dumps Spooky into Cooper's lap. "And leave a good tip. It will be mine." She darts off for the house of horror and the three of us wait a beat before continuing to inhale the lasagna. Sadly, there won't be any for dinner.

And as soon as we're through, a platter of cannolis arrives and we dive in headfirst, leaving nary a crumb behind in our wake.

"So that was fun," Niki says, patting her belly as she looks to Coop and me. "Where are we off to next?"

A tall, shirtless man slathered in green body paint struts by and Niki sits up at attention.

"Well, if it isn't the ogre of my dreams. You kids have a good time." She bolts after the jolly green giant and it's just Cooper and me.

One of us happens to be glowering at the other. I'll let you guess which one.

"Please tell me that my sister is nowhere near your suspect list," he growls.

"She's off my list if I'm off *yours*."

He gives a lopsided grin. "You found the body. I can't exclude you. It's strictly procedural."

I pick up my fork. "I'll give you a procedure."

A dull chuckle strums from him. "Remind me to watch out for you in the dark."

"We've never been in the dark."

"Maybe we should change that?" he says just as his phone chirps. He glances at the screen and sighs. "Coroner's office has Sal's report ready for me."

"I can abbreviate it for you," I offer. "He was shot with two bullets."

"True, but this will let me know if he had anything in his system. Every piece of information counts in a case like this." He gets up and I do the same.

Cooper wraps his arms around me and touches his forehead to mine. My heart pumps like mad at the thought of sharing another kiss right here under his sister's nose. And if we do, I should probably be on the lookout for stray bullets myself.

"We'll talk," he says as he takes off.

Talk?

In the dark? One can only hope.

I bite down on a smile because I do believe Cooper Knox Lazzari and I are going to find a few more things to do when the lights go out.

But for now, I'd better hightail it down to Leeds and talk to my Uncle Jimmy before my own lights go out for good.

Because as it stands, if I don't off Cooper, then it's lights out for yours truly.

CHAPTER 11

*a*fter I left the Tavern of Terror, I decided to take a detour before hitting Leeds, so I took the pooches to the dog park where they ran, jumped, and barked up a storm.

I needed to clear my head and think about what I was going to say to my uncle while I pleaded for my life and that of Cooper's. Maybe Johnny's life, too, although I probably shouldn't press my luck.

But after seeing all those other dogs all decked out for spooky season, I was starting to feel like an inadequate dog mom so I took my boys and hightailed it to the nearest pet shop and outfitted them with enough Halloween bling to terrorize any dark alley.

Watson is strutting around in a vampire cape and a cute little bowtie, looking to suck the *coos* right out of anyone with eyeballs. And Spooky has donned something akin to a polka-dotted garter belt around his neck with enough ruffles to double as a petticoat. He's supposed to be a clown, but being the true clown he is, he chewed up the rainbow wig that came with it.

At least they look festive.

It's almost evening, but I don't have it in me to call it a day. Instead, I head to the only place that can cure all my ills, my Uncle Jimmy's strip club.

I figure if I'm going to toss and turn all night about the men he wants me to off, I may as well try to negotiate my way out of the assignments.

Who knows? Maybe he'll take the hits off the table and give me something I could really sink my teeth into—a candy bar.

As much as the month of October seems to revolve around death and horror, I'm in no mood to participate. But I'll never say no to candy.

I nudge open the door to the Red Satin Gentlemen's Club and am greeted by a flood of crimson. The walls, the floor, and even the ceiling glow in that sultry hue. The music is loud and suggestive, the girls are nearly naked and *far past* suggestive, and the stench of cologne emanating from the stables of men who have shown up with cash in hand reeks of midlife crisis and desperation.

Glittering Halloween decorations adorn every corner, from glowing pumpkins to cobweb-covered chandeliers.

Watson and Spooky trot at my heels, their tails wagging excitedly as they take in the spectacle. They do their best to charge the stage, barking and yipping up a storm as they strain their leashes to capacity just trying to get their furry little mitts on those dancing dolls.

They're such boys.

The stage is a riot of color and movement, with dancers in cheesy costumes gyrating to the music. There's a witch twirling around in a sparkling black dress, a vampire queen seductively swaying in nothing but a flowing cape, and even a naughty nurse teasing the men with her stethoscope.

It's dimly lit inside, save for the dizzying swirl of lights aimed at the buxom beauties on stage, but that doesn't stop me from seeing a couple of golden oldies scarfing down a platter of nachos as if it were their last meal.

Much to the dismay of my lusty pooches, I make a beeline for the golden oldies instead.

Those oldies would be none other than Aunt Cat and Carlotta, of course. They're perched at a table near the stage, their eyes glued to the crowd in front of them as they chat away and snack on the feast set before them.

"Fancy meeting you here," I say, plopping down and helping myself to a crisp tortilla chip smothered in orange goo. My personal favorite. "Why this place?" I give the side-eye to the bride of Frankenstein who's currently disrobing on stage one strip of linen at a time.

"What's better than dinner and a show?" Carlotta shoots back. "The men watch the girls and we watch the men. It's a win-win."

Aunt Cat nods. "And there's no better eye candy than a man waving money."

"That's right." Carlotta applauds at the thought. "And the fact they're shouting *take it off* doesn't hurt either. And after they've had a few beers, they start singing that song in our direction. That's when things get *really* interesting."

"Is that why you're fueling up on nachos?" I ask, diving

back into the orange goo. "Building up your energy for later?"

"That and the fact Jimmy lets us eat for free." Aunt Cat nods.

"*Wait*, you get free food?" I balk. "But I'm family, too, and I don't have this perk."

In the least, I should get an employee discount.

"There's a reason." She wags a finger my way. "Face it, you'd eat here for breakfast, lunch, and dinner. And after falling asleep in a corner once or twice, you'd probably move in and try to live rent-free."

"Free food and free rent? Why didn't I think of that?" My eyes grow wide just as a waitress with a set of bazingas the size of watermelons delivers a fresh plate of nachos. Poor timing on my part. I think those bazingas just tattooed themselves on the inside of my eyelids. "Never mind. I don't care to look at my own bazingas let alone a new set every twenty minutes."

Both Watson and Spooky give a bark in protest and I roll my eyes. It's clear they'd trade in my rental and the dog park for this haven of naughtiness.

Aunt Cat leans in. "So how's the assignment going?"

"It's complicated," I grunt. "I haven't made a move yet."

Carlotta raises a brow. "Why the hesitation? You've got the skills, the smarts, and the bullets. What's stopping you?"

"In a word? Consequences."

Aunt Cat scoffs. "Consequences, shmonsequences. You're living the dream, Effie. Taking out the trash and getting paid for it. That boyfriend of yours is just one stripper away from being a dirty, lying, soon-to-be ex. You

ADDISON MOORE

get to cut him off at the cheating pass. What could be better?"

I shake my head. "It's a demented dream."

Carlotta tips her head my way. "But you've got to look out for number one. If your uncle says jump, you ask how high. That's the business you're in."

"Besides, we've all got our list of men we'd love to put in the crosshairs of a few bullets." Aunt Cat toasts me with a cheesy laden chip as she says it. "Remember that sleazy landlord who tried to hike up your rent last year? I bet you would have loved to pump him full of lead."

"True," I muse. "But he's not on my hit list."

She goes on. "And what about that slimy ex-boyfriend of yours? The one who cheated on you with your sister?"

"I remember," I groan at the thought. "Come to think of it, they're both lucky I didn't use them for target practice."

But for now, I'll just have to navigate the murky waters of love and duty, hoping both Cooper and I come out of it alive.

"Things are finally moving in the right direction for Cooper and me," I say. "And by right direction, I don't mean the cemetery. That man knows just what I want to hear, when I want to hear it."

"*Eh*," Carlotta grunts. "But does he know just what to do when you want it done? Now *that* might be worth keeping him out of a casket."

"We haven't got that far yet," I say. "But he did hint about doing things in the dark and I'm pretty sure he didn't mean while buried six feet under."

Aunt Cat waves me off. "The dark is overrated. Find

64

yourself a man who isn't afraid to show his moves with the lights on."

"Yeah, but I'm more of a lights-off kind of a girl," I say. "You know, to keep the mystery alive." And keep the fact my bazingas are starting to take a road trip to my navel. A secret I'll take to the grave.

As if on cue, the lights and the music cut out as the entire facility is plunged into darkness.

Hey? Maybe the women here are thinking the same thing.

"Welcome to the dance of doom," a deep, disembodied voice warbles from the speakers and the crowd goes wild. I never said they were smart. "But beware—for the night is young, and the shadows hold a secret darker than the grave. And for some of you, this night might just be your last dance."

That's exactly what I'm afraid of.

Within seconds, red and pink lights swirl around the stage in spasms as the music kicks in again. And soon, a whole new group of women dressed as naughty princesses and frisky fairies trots onto the stage. Every last one of them is waving a sparkling wand that glows in the dark, and that's all it takes for Watson and Spooky to lose their furry little minds.

Their leashes slip from my grasp so abruptly I'm positive if I had wrapped them around my wrists I would have lost both hands.

The next thing I know, they're on stage and quickly snapped up by two of the dancers, gyrating and swinging their hips with the pups in tow.

ADDISON MOORE

Men flock their way as if the dogs themselves were the true siren song.

Money flies.

Men howl.

Dogs bark.

And the beer is flowing.

I'm starting to think I should demand my cut.

Soon, Watson and Spooky have enough bills tucked around their collars to send my future kids to college, and yet I know I won't see a dime.

It's nice to know someone in the family has the Midas touch when it comes to scraping up a dollar.

"Hey, do you think I could bust a naughty move like that?" I muse. "Those are my dogs. I should be raking in the big bucks," I say, shoving another cheese-filled chip into my piehole as I contemplate a career as a doggie dancer.

"*Nah.*" Aunt Cat doesn't waste any time in killing my dreams. "If you were up there shaking your stuff, people might think you were having a medical issue. Face it, you might have the goods, but you don't have the moves. Those women are trained professionals. Do not try this at home."

For as long as I can remember, my rebellious spirit has had more to do with proving others wrong than it ever did with me wanting to fly in the face of authority.

I make a beeline for the stage and hop right on it before I can talk myself out of it, and then my hips are bucking, my chest is flapping, and I'm doing my best to give myself whiplash.

"*Stop the show,*" one of the girls calls out and the house lights flick on, breaking the sultry spell as the music cuts out, killing the sultry mood.

The next thing I know, I'm being held down by four buxom beauties with their bazingas swinging like pendulums.

"Do we have a doctor in the house?" one of them shouts. "This woman is having a seizure!"

And just like that, my career as a dancer is over before it ever began.

Not even a cute little pooch could have saved me.

I guess I'd better stick to what I'm good at.

Scratch that.

I'd better stick to what I'm decidedly below average at.

Speaking of which, it's time to do what I came for—talk to Uncle Jimmy.

CHAPTER 12

Once the EMTs give me the proper medical clearance, I grab my furry little besties and head straight for the heart of this denizen of sin—the illegal gambling casino in the basement.

I never said my uncle was a saint.

The air in the basement is heavy with the scent of stale cigarette smoke and the hint of cheap liquor. The casino itself is dimly lit yet spacious and seems to go on an entire football field. It wouldn't surprise me one bit to find out that my uncle hollowed out half of Leeds to make all of his dicey dreams come true.

It holds all of the glitz and glamour of a Vegas casino, if that casino paid out poorly and was run by the mob.

Rows and rows of one-armed bandits line the place, glittering, whistling, and pulsating—just begging to suck the life right out of your wallet.

There's a smattering of roulette tables, several dozen poker and blackjack tables, and the requisite booze station is set up every three feet.

And let's not forget the throngs of people. The hopes and dreams of these poor souls might bring them through the door, but it's the booze that keeps the money flowing—right out of the wallets of these greedy fools.

Speaking of greedy fools, I pluck a few quarters out of my pocket—the sum total income of my short-lived career as a stripper—and drop it into a winking, blinking machine that holds the promise of a triple seven.

"All right, boys," I say to the cute pooches that I'm holding hostage in my arms. "Rub a paw over the beast for good luck. Mama needs a brand new bag—that I can potentially hock and retire off of." Both Watson and Spooky do their thing, aka slobbering like a couple of pros. They had a lot of practice upstairs, and I no sooner pull the handle than I hear what sounds like a seal barking in the next row over.

I crane my neck that way just as a bell goes off and I spot a dark-haired woman in a hot pink tracksuit clapping and whooping it up as the lights spasm at the slot machine in front of her. And just as she's swarmed by an entire gaggle of employees, I gasp at the sight. But it's not the fact she's just won a thousand dollars according to the blinking sign above her head that has me astonished. It's the fact Loretta the Black Widow Lazzari is just a few feet away—striking it rich in Canelli country no less.

I cast a rueful glance back at my coin-hungry machine as it does its best to shake me down once again and instead, I shake my head in dismay.

I'd better boot-scoot out of this place before Loretta spots me and runs straight to Cooper with the latest gossip. The last thing I need is Cooper putting two and two together before we can put one and one together—as in *ourselves*. And speaking of which, if I don't get his name crossed off my hit list, it will be one and *none*.

I hightail it to a series of darkened hallways to the left, and that dark and depressing labyrinth eventually leads to the scariest room of them all in this morally bankrupt place—my uncle's office.

After tap-dancing around a couple of his henchmen, begging them not to shoot, and tossing my surname around as if it were an FBI badge, I finally get in.

The office is small and boxy. It has all of the appeal of the inside of a metal filing cabinet and is about as roomy as a coffin. You'd think a guy as rich as Jimmy would be seated on a fourteen-karat gold throne—in the form of a toilet due to his bladder issues—but nonetheless, my uncle is a man of simple needs. Or just plain poor decorating skills.

Uncle Jimmy is perched behind a big desk veiled from the smoke of his cigar, looking every bit like someone who wouldn't hesitate to pluck your heart out and stick it on a cupcake. In that sense, he's got a lot in common with Lottie—at least during this time of year.

He's sitting under the one and only light in this abysmal hovel, and oddly enough it gives him the appeal of an angel of light. Yet everyone knows the devil was once an angel, and I'm starting to think his name was Jimmy Canelli.

He's old as dirt, has a head of thick gray hair, and dark empty eyes to match his soul.

"Bella facia." He offers me the same greeting he has since I was a kid. Come to think of it, he greets my sisters the exact same way. I bet it really cut down on having to remember any of our names. "What's this? Another dog?" He motions for me to hand them over and I let them loose on the desk.

Both Watson and Spooky trot his way and lick his face silly until he's giggling like a schoolgirl.

Traitors.

Although it might be wise to get him in a good mood, and what better way to do it than with some canine lovin'? If that doesn't work, I know a naughty nurse upstairs who could do things with a stethoscope that were so impressive, ten different men emptied out their 401K and tucked it into her uniform. And once she donned those latex gloves, they emptied out their wife's 401K, too.

"What can I do for you?" he asks with that dreamy look only a couple of puppies could provide.

"Why does Cooper have to go?" I decide to cut right to the chase before one of the dogs does his business on top of Jimmy's lap. I figure I'm on a timer in that department. Seeing that it takes place regularly when we're at home, it's destined to happen. As cute as those little furry faces are, they're nothing but ticking time bombs when it comes to peppering the place with their special little brownies.

"He's onto us." Uncle Jimmy frowns as if he isn't happy about it either.

"He's not onto us. He's more in love with me than ever before."

A part of me wants to offer to take down every other Lazzari in exchange for him. But even attempting that would set off a turf war like no other. And yet I happen to think Cooper is worth a turf war or two.

"Effie." He rolls his eyes.

So he does know my name—and apparently, how exasperating I can be.

"He's a cop," he continues. "He's one of them. To top it off, he's a Lazzari. I don't care how many times he changes his last name, he can't change the fact he's blood from the same bowl."

Eww.

As much as I'd like to insist that Coop has nothing to do with his looney tunes family, the head looney tune of the Lazzari clan is sitting no less than fifty feet away collecting cold, hard Canelli-issued cash to the tune of one grand. And Cooper just so happens to have a heart for her.

And I just so happen to have a heart for Cooper.

Oh, what a twisted web we weave when first we practice to off a few people for some government-issued lettuce.

"Which brings me to my next point," I say, brazenly unfinished with my last. "Johnny the Meatball Marino's brother dropped dead last night. We can't off Johnny or we'll be offing his mother by proxy."

Sure, Aunt Cat already told me that he's well aware, but I figure it couldn't hurt to drive the point home.

Uncle Jimmy's eyes turn a strange shade of red. Come to think of it, his entire countenance glows with the unholy hue.

Looks like I was right about that devil thing because I can almost see his horns sprouting.

"That no-good-for-nothing weasel should have thought about that before taking off with a pile of my money and giving me the finger once my men showed up to collect."

"Maybe he was just trying to point out that he needed another minute?" I cringe as the words leave my mouth.

"He was pointing out that he likes to dance with death." He leans my way and looks every bit like the son of perdition—if the son of perdition wore a gold rope necklace with a gold horn dangling from it. An obvious ode to his homeland, and I'm not talking about Italy.

"That boy is one dead meatball," he growls. "And so is the Lazzari with the badge. If you don't take care of business by midnight next Tuesday, it'll be my business to take care of you. As much as it pains me, Bella, the only way out of this is through a casket. Now whose body is going to lie in it? Theirs or yours?"

"Yours," I say, jumping out of my seat and he reaches for his weapon. "GAH! I mean *theirs*."

Grammar isn't exactly my strong suit while my life is on the line.

"Don't you worry," I say, scooping up fuzzy Thing One and furry Thing Two—hoping Jimmy won't notice the puddle Thing Two just left on his desk. "I'll have those men dead and delivered straight to the morgue by midnight next Tuesday." I pause at the door. "Why next Tuesday?"

He shrugs. "It's Halloween. I'd like to think of it as my contribution to the great beyond in honor of All Souls' Day."

"How charitable of you." I lift a puppy as if to toast him and a trail of tinkle rains from his hind end.

"*Leave*, before your luck runs out," Uncle Jimmy shouts and I run all the way out of the dark labyrinth of hallways, only to smack right into a hot pink Italian princess who just so happens to be one grand richer.

Would you look at that?
My luck just ran out.

CHAPTER 13

I begged and pleaded and assured Loretta that I'd be willing to do anything if she just kept her bloated lips sealed—including letting her get away with murder.

Okay, I didn't say anything of that. I told her my uncle wanted a box of Lottie's donuts delivered fresh—devil's food to be exact. And upon hearing it, she said she had a sudden hankering for devil's food herself.

Figures.

She took off to hunt down a donut and I took off to hunt down a killer.

Okay, so I went home, fed the pooches, and snored violently until morning.

I can only handle so much excitement for one day.

The next morning, I worked my shift at the bakery until four, ate enough glazed crullers to qualify as breakfast, lunch, and dinner, then picked up my pooches and decided to check out the Halloween Spooktacular Fall Festival down at the fairgrounds.

Watson and Spooky hop and yip, as cheery as can be as soon as we arrive.

A gust of cold, crisp fall air greets me, sending shivers down my spine. Dark clouds loom overhead, casting a shadow over the festivities, which seems on par considering the nature of the celebration.

The fairgrounds are a kaleidoscope of colors—mostly orange, black, and purple—while a canopy of twinkle lights shines from above, and there are rows and rows of booths adorned with Halloween decorations.

The place is thick with bodies. The air is alive with excitement and filled with the sound of laughter, as children run from one attraction to the next. Creepy mood music plays over the speakers, and the scent of popcorn and cotton candy wafts through the air, mingling with the aroma of pumpkin spice and caramel apples.

In other words, it's heaven—even if it is mostly disguised as the hot place.

Stalls are decorated with jack-o'-lanterns and skeletons, while ghostly figures dance on strings above the crowds. The Ferris wheel stands tall against the ever-darkening sky, its neon lights flashing bright. The games on the midway are in full swing, with a whole gaggle of teens trying their luck at winning stuffed animals the size of a refrigerator.

Food stands line the pathways, offering an array of treats ranging from hot cider and funnel cakes, to deep-fried candy bars and corn dogs. I'm pretty sure I'm going to hit all of the above. The scent of sizzling sausages and roasted nuts fills the air, tempting me in their direction as well with their savory aromas.

"What should we try first?" I ask as the dogs bark and dance. "How about one of those giant soft pretzels? That way we can share."

Who am I kidding? I'm getting three. With four siblings, I've already shared one too many times.

Once I flew the coop, I vowed never to share a single thing again. Apparently, that includes my body, but that was sort of inadvertent. There haven't been any decent prospects. Not until Cooper, at least.

The three of us navigate the crowd and get in a line twenty deep at the soft pretzel stand. You'd think they were giving away free beer the way the throngs have flocked to this locale. But then, these twisted beauties are fresh baked, so I can't really blame anyone for sticking it out. And with just one more person ahead of us, we're about to make all of our pretzel dreams come true right up until I spot my next suspect walking by briskly and dipping into the crowd.

"Oh, for Pete's sake," I chuff as I wage how long the person in front of me will be before glancing back in the crowd as Johnny the Meatball Marino's dark hair quickly fades out of sight. "Sorry, boys. Duty calls," I say and they both give an exasperated bark as I do my best to tug them away from pretzel heaven. "We'll come back, I promise."

We dart into the crowd, and as if they know the way, Watson and Spooky propel me through the melee amidst the hustle and bustle.

As I weave through the crowds, my heart quickens at the sight of seeing Johnny the Meatball Marino in the wild. I can't believe he's here, swaggering through the fairgrounds like he owns the place, oblivious to the fact that his time is up.

Lucky for me, I have my weapon tucked in my purse. Although, lucky for Johnny, I'm not opening fire in a crowd of thousands.

We follow along as he ducks behind a row of booths and makes contact with each of the vendors along the midway. He keeps digging into his coat pocket and pulling out a wad of something small, not green enough to be cash, and handing it over as he travels from booth to booth repeating the effort.

Once he reaches the end of the line, he takes off and strays into a clearing before heading for the woods.

"Where the heck is he going?" I ask as we try our best to follow behind. I watch as he ducks into the forest, away from the crowds, away from prying eyes, and leans against an evergreen as he fiddles with his phone.

"Here's my chance," I pant as we veer to the left and sneak up within spitting distance.

My heart begins to race as the obvious becomes apparent. There's not a soul around. And he's practically taunting me to nick him with a bullet. And that's exactly what I'm planning to do.

Watson and Spooky curl up around my feet and promptly take a nap while I riffle through my purse, praying to high heaven that I brought my silencer along. As boisterous as that fall festival is, someone out there will be able to identify a gunshot.

And sure enough, I have it! I quickly place it over my Glock as my heart thunders in my chest.

This is it.

With my weapon at the ready and Watson and Spooky at my side, I circle around my mark. Johnny shifts and turns his back to me, so I take a deep breath and steady my aim.

The air grows thick with anticipation as I raise my weapon.

Here goes nothing. But just as I'm about to pull the trigger, a sudden pang of guilt grips me.

Do I really have the heart to send yet another Marino to the pearly gates? Sure, I didn't off Sal. But if I kill Johnny, I'll be killing his mother as well.

I can't do it.

I lower my weapon a notch just as Watson and Spooky jerk at the sound of a chipmunk nearby, and before I know it, each one wraps themselves around a different leg and I'm being pulled apart like a wishbone.

A scream evicts from me, my finger squeezes the trigger, and Johnny dances a jig in front of me.

"What the heck?" He barrels my way and I quickly slip my weapon back into my purse just as he tackles me to the ground. "Get down," he shouts as he covers me with his body. "There's a shooter out here somewhere."

"There is?" I cautiously open an eye as I glance up at him. "I mean, there *is*," I say, thankfully he has no clue that the shooter was me. And how kind of him to offer to lay down his life for mine, never mind the fact he just got to second base. "I think they're gone now."

"How do you know?" he asks gruffly, his head still on a swivel.

"Because I don't hear any gunfire," I say, shoving him off of me.

"They were using a silencer," he grunts as he helps me to my feet. "What are you doing out here?"

"The same thing you're doing out here," I say. "Trying to find some peace. That Halloween monster mash isn't for the faint of heart." I motion toward the commotion and he nods.

"Same. I'm not here for the thrills. I was just dropping off some coupons for the new restaurant I just opened with my brother, God rest his soul."

I feign shock. "Sal the Sausage was your brother?" Even though we were introduced that night, I doubt he recognizes me without my bunny ears.

He gives a subtle nod as if he were hesitant to admit it.

"I'm so sorry for your loss. I've been to the Tavern of Terror. You've got a real hit on your hands. Your lasagna and meatball with marinara beats out Mangias. But don't tell them I said so."

He belts out a belly laugh and wraps an arm around my shoulders as we make our way out of the woods and into the clearing.

"You're my new best friend," he says. "And look at these guys." He bends over and gives the boys some loving.

"She's your new best friend?" a deep voice emanates from behind, and just as I turn around, the dogs go wild.

"Come here, boys," Cooper says as they run into his arms and he scoops them up.

"Cooper?" I straighten at the sight of him. "What are you doing here?"

"You have impeccable timing, Officer," Johnny says as we step his way.

"*Detective*. And it's nice seeing you again." He frowns my way. "It's nice seeing you again, too."

I bet. I frown right back.

"You won't believe what just happened," Johnny pants as he casts a glance back into the woods. "Someone just popped off a shot our way."

"A *what?*" Cooper's voice hikes a notch just as both dogs lick his face at once, and I'll admit, it's an adorable look.

"As in bullets." Johnny nods. "They were coming from the woods. As soon I turned around, I saw this sweet thing walking her dogs, so I jumped right on her. You know, to protect her."

"*Aww*," I coo. "He called me sweet."

Cooper's eyes flit my way and he's still frowning. "So sweet," he says it, but I can tell he doesn't mean it. "I'll call it in, Johnny. I'll have the security beefed up at the fair, too." Cooper makes a quick call and then shoves his phone back into his pocket. "Any news on who could have shot your brother?"

Johnny ticks his head to the side. "No news on my part, but if those bullets are any indication, I think the killer is after me, too." He sheds a short-lived smile. "It sounds like you might have your work cut out for you. Loretta and I are happy you're on the case. You're like family to me now." He gives Cooper a mock sock to the arm. "If I can help at all, just let me know." He starts to take off and I scramble in his direction.

"Wait," I say as I catch up to him. "There was a dark-haired man having it out with Sal the night he was killed. He was tall, had dark eyes, and was brooding. Any idea who he could be?"

"I know exactly who he is." Johnny's expression darkens as he casts a glance at the festivities. "Sergio Sorrentino. He's a part owner at Mangias. The guy's a dirtbag." He nods back to Coop then me. "Have a good night. Stay safe." He takes off and quickly disappears into the crowd.

"Welp." I turn to face Cooper. "It's just you and me."

He nods my way with a stone-cold expression. "And a madman or madwoman with bullets."

Why do I get the feeling I'm in trouble?

CHAPTER 14

"*E*ffie, what the heck are you doing out here?" Cooper's voice is sharp and his tone is laced with irritation.

I'll admit, it's a good look on him. He's traded his suit for jeans and a flannel, his shiny black shoes for a pair of sneakers, and it's the kind of dress code that makes me want to pull him into the woods and have my way with him.

I'm not sure why, but I'm pretty sure that's the dress code of every bad boy I've ever known, and deep down, I've always had a soft spot for bad boys. And with all that Lazzari blood running through his veins, Cooper is as bad as bad can be.

"It's not what it looks like," I say just as both Watson and Spooky turn my way and whimper as if to protest the lie because it's exactly what it looks like.

The Halloween Harvest Festival is in full swing to our left, but Cooper and I are across a clearing and next to a thicket of evergreens threatening to swallow us whole in the night. The air is crisp, the food smells heavenly, and the chaos from the crowd is essentially echoing what's going on inside my head. "I was just taking the pooches for a walk." More whimpering ensues.

Have I mentioned they're a couple of furry little traitors?

"A walk, really?" Cooper tips his head, looking not all that impressed with the direction I've chosen to take the conversation. "Because from where I'm standing, it looks like you're cozying up to a suspect in the middle of what could potentially be a brand new crime scene."

"So you'll admit, Johnny the Meatball Marino is a suspect!"

"Everyone who showed up at *that* crime scene is a suspect in my book."

I inch back and gag. "Are we back to this again? You don't really think I'm a cold-blooded killer, do you?"

He lifts a brow and looks ten times more handsome.

Darn those dark wooly brows of his.

"Are you?" he asks point-blank and it's like a shot to the heart. Mostly because he's forcing my hand and I'm about to dole out another half-truth.

"No," I shoot back.

"What were you really doing out here with Johnny?"

"You know me, always looking for new friends in all the wrong places."

"Okay." Cooper's jaw clenches, and I can see the frustration written on his face. "This isn't a joke, Effie. You could have gotten yourself killed—or worse, compromised the investigation. I don't need you quizzing any potential suspect for me. I can handle things from here on out."

"That might be so, but I got him to give us another clue. We have to speak to Sergio. I saw him having it out with Sal before someone pumped him full of bullets."

My purse suddenly feels like a glowing hot potato as it clings to my side because, let's face it, I'm in the woods with another man who just so happens to be on my hit list and my gun is perfectly fitted with a silencer.

Although this is Cooper we're talking about. He's trained to fire back. I'd hate for Watson to see his parents fighting it out with bullets. Spooky, on the other hand, would probably get a thrill out of it. He's weird that way.

"I'll take care of Sergio." He glowers at me as the dogs nearly leap from his arms and I scoop up their leashes. "And just to be clear, I knew he had it out with Sal that night because I reviewed the security footage."

"You did?" I gasp as I step his way. "So did you see who killed Sal?"

"No. The path leading to the alley didn't have a camera pointed at it."

"I bet the killer knew that! And by the way, I had no clue about the security cameras at all, so I guess that means you can safely rule me out."

"I'm not ruling you out of anything, sweetheart." His lips curve with the hint of a dangerous smile and it makes my insides explode with heat. "You're a walking, talking ball of trouble, Effie. This is your last warning and it's for your own good. Stay away from my suspects."

"Okay, fine," I say with all the drama of a petulant child. "But don't blame me if I bump into Sergio while I'm hunting down a killer pizza at Mangias."

"You're impossible."

"Some might say it's one of my finer traits," I shoot back. No one would say that, but they would agree with him without hesitation.

Watson and Spooky begin to yip and bark and dance in a circle like the furry cutie pies they are.

Cooper takes the leashes from me as he offers them both a hearty scratch.

"By the way, you do realize you had the dogs out here. You could have put them in harm's way, too."

A smidge of guilt creeps in. I did misfire my weapon and things could have gone horribly wrong.

"It's not my fault," I'm quick to say and slow to believe. "They've gotten into the habit of following me wherever I go. But don't worry, they weren't in any danger. They're more like my furry bodyguards."

"Furry bodyguards, huh?" He raises a brow once again and my insides go wild. If one more stray eyebrow goes rogue, I might be moved to try to get him to cuddle in the woods with me, naked. "Let's hope they're better at guarding than you are at staying out of trouble."

"Hey, I'll have you know that Watson here has a mean bark. And Spooky? He's got a killer cuddle game."

I hike my own brow his way and hope he takes the hint. Naked cuddling is still very much on the table for me.

Cooper shakes his head. "Just keep an eye on them, okay? We don't need any more things going wrong this month."

"Got it." I nod, feeling a pang of guilt for putting the dogs in harm's way—*my* way to be exact. "I'll make sure they stay out of trouble." Or at least try to.

His chest expands the size of the woods before he lets out a sigh.

"You know"—he says with a mischievous glint in his eye—"I heard the real reason people come to places like this is to load up on junk food. Could that have been your true intent all along?"

I scoff, pretending to take offense. "Hey, I'll have you know that I came here for the haunted atmosphere, the scary excitement—and maybe just a little bit for the deep-fried Oreos."

There is no greater truth.

Cooper Knox Lazzari really does have my number. I guess he's a pretty good detective after all.

"I hear they have a mean funnel cake," he says. "How about it? Are you in?"

I grin, unable to resist the temptation. "Well, maybe just one. Or two. Okay, fine, I'll admit it, I came here to indulge in all the guilty delicious pleasures this twisted harvest festival has to offer. But hey, you can't blame a girl for wanting to treat herself every now and then, right?" More like every few hours when it comes to me. "I bet I can out-eat you in the junk food department."

"I'd like to see you try. Just don't come crying to me when you're about to fall into a sugar coma."

"Some white and shining knight you are," I nudge him with my elbow as we start to head for the fairgrounds. "I'll have you know that I have the metabolism of a cheetah. Nothing can slow me down."

And nothing does. Cooper and I start off with four soft, warm pretzels, one for each of us, including our hungry doggies. We move on to the deep-fried Snickers, then the deep-fried sticks of butter—yes, that happened—cookies of every iteration, corn dogs that I'll dream about for years to come, and everything else they've managed to stick in a fryer. I may or may not have eaten a button. It was so-so.

Eventually, we round things off with the aforementioned funnel cake, the caramel apple nachos, and some pumpkin spice hand pies in the shape of a jack-o'-lantern with the face cut out into a goofy little grin.

"What now?" I say, holding my stomach as Watson and Spooky strain at their leashes, eager to run through the crowd of teenagers dressed as slutty princesses and ghoulish jocks.

"It looks like those two still have some energy to burn," he says before locking his gaze to mine. "How about I take us on a hot date you will never forget?"

My insides ignite once again as if a nuclear warhead just went off in my stomach, although that might just be the corn dog talking.

"A hot date I will never forget? How can I say no to that? Your place or mine?"

"Let's just say it's a place we'll both take up residence at eventually. And beware, it has the power to scare the socks right off of you."

Fair warning—we can start with taking my socks off, but with Cooper looking like my favorite sin tonight, the rest of my clothes won't be far behind either.

CHAPTER 15

"The cemetery?" I balk as we file out of our cars, and I take a look at the place Cooper has dragged me off to for our so-called hot date.

Although to be fair, he did say this place could scare the socks right off of me. But still, not the aphrodisiac I was hoping for.

Honey Hollow Cemetery sprawls before us, shrouded in a misty veil of the dead and the damned. Tombstones jut out from the ground like crooked teeth, casting long shadows in the fading light of the moon. Wisps of fog snake among the graves, lending this place the exact otherworldly charm it deserves.

Watson and Spooky wiggle and jiggle, excited to be at what they probably think is another dog park—the exception being this place has a lot more bones.

A throng of bodies, all of them upright and moving, chat away to the right, and there's a woman decked out like Morticia Addams holding a lantern that glows red as she prattles on about something to the crowd.

"Welcome to the Graveyard Jaunt," Cooper says with a touch of pride. "Looks like we made it just in time for the nightly tour of all things haunted. I've always wanted to do one of these but was too afraid to do it on my own."

"So he lies, too," I say to the dogs and Cooper rumbles with a laugh.

People are milling about, dressed in an array of creepy costumes that range from ghoulish ghosts to sinister clowns. The air is alive with the chatter of excited thrill-seekers, eager to embark on the Halloween tour of the cemetery. And, sure enough, there's a large sign set up on a tripod with glowing green letters that reads, *Welcome to the Honey Hollow Haunted Graveyard Jaunt! Please leave a donation in our tip jar! Or risk being haunted for life.*

The tip jar set at the base of it glows, too—or more to the point, the skull sitting inside of it is shining like a jack-o'-lantern.

"I don't know about this," I shiver as I say it. "I'm not exactly dressed for a night among the dead."

"Ah, come on, Effie." Cooper flashes a devilish grin my way as he takes up my hand. "You're going to love it. And besides, you've got me to protect you."

My lips press tight as a jolt travels up my arm as his hand warms mine.

"And who's going to protect you?" I tease.

"What do you think we brought the dogs for?"

Cooper leads us onto the grounds as we do our best not to step on any of the granite grave markers, but with the way Watson and Spooky stop off at every other one to tinkle, you'd think they were aiming for the poor souls.

Although, after all I've done in my life, I'd probably deserve a tinkle or two on my grave.

Despite my reservations, Cooper leads the way and soon we come upon a makeshift stand offering haunted hot chocolate. The entire setup is adorable, with its purple and green twinkle lights wrapped around it, and the three women working the stand look as if they've just stepped out of a crypt themselves with their hair white as snow and scraggly, their pale faces and dark gaunt eyes. But those dusty, musty period dresses they've donned with the high collars and full bustles look simply to die for and something tells me they might have done just that.

The line moves quickly as the scent of warm cocoa and spices wafts toward us, mingling with the crisp autumn air. Soon enough, Cooper pays up and we're both holding a hot cup of chocolate dreams in our cold little hands, complete with a dollop of whipped cream and a sprinkle of cinnamon.

"Just what we need to warm up," I say as I take a sip of the rich, velvety liquid warming me from the inside out. "*Mmm*, this is delicious."

"Glad you like it," he says, wrapping an arm around my shoulder and once again I'm warmed from head to toe. "Now, let's go see what Honey Hollow Cemetery has in store for us. Who knows what spooky surprises await us in the darkened corners of the graveyard?"

"Detective?" a disembodied female voice chirps from our left and I look that way and frown.

"Speaking of spooky surprises," I mutter as Naomi Turner makes her presence known. She's decked out as a vampire, complete with a luscious black satin cape with red velvet lining, and what looks to be a French maid's uniform underneath that. And for once she has her head sitting right where it's supposed to be.

"Well, well, well, look who's haunting the graveyard tonight?" I sneer at her. "How about showing off your brand new party trick and taking your head off its base?" And as soon as she does, I'll show off my soccer skills and kick it right into Leeds. But with my luck, Watson and Spooky would chase after it and bring it right back.

"Hello, Detective Knox," Naomi purrs, ignoring my charming segue into polite evening chatter. "Fancy meeting you here." Naomi takes a moment to gesture at my attire. "I didn't realize they were casting for a B horror flick. It's practically typecasting with you, Effie."

"I know what *you're* here for," I say, gesturing to her attire as well. "Just another trampy vamp yearning for a moment in the moonlight. You can go home. They're not casting triple X films in this place either."

"I'm here for the haunted tour," she spits my way.

I liked her better with her head off its base. And if she keeps snipping at me, that can be arranged.

"Well, we're here because we're on a hot date," I say, not hesitating to link my arm to Cooper's.

"Bringing a lady to a haunted graveyard tour?" Naomi chortles. "How positively romantic." She winks his way, undeterred by my presence—or that fact we're connected like a couple of Lego pieces. Naomi's flirtation clearly knows no bounds.

Cooper chuckles. "What could be more fun?"

I can think of a few things, and I'm pretty sure they're illegal to do in a cemetery. Just my luck again.

"Well, count me in on the fun," Naomi says, wiggling her chest his way. "My sister, Keelie, and her husband talked me into coming with them. But I was starting to feel like a third wheel." She cozies up on the other side of Coop. "Thank goodness I ran into you."

"Because nothing says not a third wheel like crashing a hot date," I mutter.

"Oh hush, you," she's quick to reprimand me. "Who could blame me for not wanting to miss out on the chance to spend time with such a strong, handsome man who can protect me from all the spooky ghouls and ghosts."

"Yeah, but who's going to protect you from me?" I'm only half-teasing. If we happen to come upon a freshly dug hole in the ground, not even Cooper can stop me from giving the wench a good shove.

And if he's a smart man, he'll pick up a shovel and help keep her there.

The woman leading the tour is dressed as if she stepped right out of some long ago haunted era herself, complete with a flowing gown that looks as if it's made of gossamer, long black hair that's frayed at the edges, a deathly pale face, and blood red lips that gleam with a wicked smile.

She introduces herself as Madame Morticia—knew it—and quickly welcomes us to the Honey Hollow Haunted Graveside Jaunt where she assures us we'll be stumbling upon the dead and asks us not to break a hip while we're at it.

I glance over at Naomi and glower. I'd like to break something, all right.

"Welcome, dear souls"—Morticia continues—"to the most ghoulish graveyard ghost walk you will ever embark on. Tonight, we journey through the shadows of time, where love and loss intertwine like vines upon a tombstone. Are you ready to unravel the mysteries that linger in the whispers of the night?" She raises a hand dramatically and unleashes a glitter bomb that has half the crowd gasping with delight. "Our first tale takes us to the forlorn grave of Lady Genevieve, whose heartache echoes through the ages. Legend has it that her spirit still roams these grounds, searching for her lost love. Alas, some poor souls are simply doomed to walk the planet alone."

I give Naomi a look and her mouth rounds out in horror.

"You wish," she hisses my way while linking her own arm to Cooper as well.

I'll give her a pass, considering we're traversing the crypts with the cryptkeeper herself. But as soon as we're back in the land of the living, I just might use her for target practice.

"But beware, dear travelers"—Morticia says as she leads us deeper into the realm of the dead—"for not all love stories have a happy ending. Some are tinged with betrayal and deceit, like the tragic tale of George and Grimilda, whose love turned to madness and murder."

I nod. "Now that's something I can sink my teeth into."

"Easy, girl," Cooper says and sets my insides on fire once again.

Who knew Cooper in a cemetery could get me going?

Me. That's who.

Now if I can only put Naomi Turner some place where she can't bother the two of us.

I slice her a dark look that suggests I'm about to do just that.

CHAPTER 16

The tour moves on and soon we're knee-deep in tombstones and even Watson and Spooky seem to be shivering with fear.

"Now where were we?" Madame Morticia looks momentarily stymied by what she's doing in a cemetery. "Oh yes, the tragic tale of George and Grimilda, whose love turned to madness and murder."

"Love and murder?" Naomi whispers our way. "That sounds like Loretta Lazzari's last six marriages."

Cooper's muscles go rigid and my jaw goes slack.

I bet Naomi has no clue that Loretta the Black Widow Lazzari is Cooper's little sister. Ha! For once I'm happy that Naomi's head is screwed on straight tonight. Now we can watch as she hangs herself.

Now that would be all treat and no tricks.

She leans toward Cooper. "I bet they're giving Loretta a frequent buyer's discount at this place. What do you think?"

"I think Loretta has only been married twice," he points

out and his jaw cinches as if he were stopping himself from saying something more—and most likely a touch more colorful.

Come to think of it, Cooper is probably an expert at holding it together when it comes to the topic of his sister. He's had to deal with her shenanigans for a lifetime.

"*Please.*" Naomi is quick to discredit his expertise on the topic. "Who knows how many dead husbands that Italian female stallion has stashed away."

Ha! She doesn't realize Cooper is *Italian* either.

Strike *two.*

"I bet she's putting all of the funeral expenses on her credit card and racking up some serious travel miles." Naomi tightens the noose around her neck and I can't help but smile. "But then, she won't need to take a plane anywhere. I've seen the broomstick she rides in on." And just like that, she's kicked out the chair beneath her.

I can't help but chuckle and Cooper shoots me a look.

"I wasn't laughing at that," I tell him. "I was laughing at *that.*" I point to the walking tramp stamp among us—Naomi herself.

Madame Morticia gestures toward a looming mausoleum. "And here lies the final resting place of the infamous Widow's Curse."

Naomi giggles like a schoolgirl. "I knew we'd stumble upon Loretta's crypt eventually. It's nice to know she's corralled them all in one place."

Just like Naomi is corralling herself to a certain doom.

And I don't mind one bit.

I think, I can honestly say, I've never been so glad to have her around.

Morticia waves a glowing arm at the spectacle before us. "Legend has it that the Black Widow in question had so many husbands, her tombstone doubles as a scoreboard."

Naomi leans in. "You'd better watch it, Coop. Word on the street is Loretta is looking for her next victim."

"Don't worry," Coop says dryly. "She's not my type."

I can't help but snicker. I'm glad he didn't out the fact she's his sibling. I'd hate to turn off the horror show that Naomi is putting on so soon. Who knew she could provide such ripe entertainment?

We continue with the tour as Madame Morticia regales us with tales of ghostly apparitions, unrequited love, and mysterious disappearances as her voice carries an eerie cadence that seems to echo through the tombstones.

"And so"—Morticia concludes while veiled in an air of mystery, or it could be the cigarette smoke from the ghoul to our left—"I encourage you all to explore the realm of the dead on your own. But remember, tread lightly, for the spirits that dwell here may not take kindly to unwelcome guests."

With those cryptic words hanging in the air, Morticia bids us farewell, disappearing into the shadows as though she were but a phantom herself.

I slice a glance at my own unwelcomed guest just as someone whistles from across the way. It's Keelie, and she's waving her sister in that direction as if she were landing a 747.

"That's my ride," Naomi snips. "It was nice spending time with you." She caresses Cooper's cheek with her glowing blue fingers. I'm not too worried. She probably takes them off at night just like her head. "Don't forget, the

Tavern of Terror is having a big bash on Halloween night. I expect you to be there."

"I wouldn't miss it," he says.

"And you won't want to miss what I'm wearing," she purrs. "Or more to the point, what I won't be wearing." She winks before slinking off in the dark.

"I don't know what she's wearing for Halloween," I say. "But I do know what she's wearing tonight—her *foot* in her mouth. Sorry about all those cracks she made about your sister. At least you got to see Naomi's true colors in action."

"And what about your true colors?" He hitches a brow.

"What about them?"

"I don't know"—he takes a look around—"we're in a cemetery. I was just thinking that a thoughtful woman like you might be moved to tears at the brevity of life, and how precious each and every day is." He shrugs. "What am I saying? You're the kindest soul I know. You wouldn't want a single person to land here, let alone land here well before their time."

Before I can process his words, both Watson and Spooky drag me off to the right and soon the four of us are miles from any living being—and alone, with this entire side of the darkened cemetery to ourselves.

I'll have to remember to reward these frisky pooches with a few extra doggie treats when we get home.

Some alone time with the good detective is treat enough for me.

"Now"—I say, wrapping my arms around the hottie in the flannel—"let's see what your true colors are, Detective."

A malevolent smile tugs at his lips as he inches his head toward mine, and just as he comes within striking range, a disembodied moan rides through the air and it sounds decidedly female.

"What was that?" I ask, clamping onto Coop so tight you couldn't squeeze a dime between us.

The moaning strikes again, this time twice as loud—and with another far more masculine voice added to the choir.

The atmosphere grows heavy with a sense of foreboding, and even Cooper seems slow to explore the vicinity.

Watson and Spooky race to my right as their leashes slip right through my frightened fingers and just like that Cooper and I are traversing headstones with the best of them in an effort to catch up.

They stop cold in front of a tombstone, and just as I'm about to take another step in their direction, a pale hand flops onto the grass.

I scream.

Cooper screams.

And the next thing you know, a man and a woman spike up half-dressed from behind that tombstone, screaming up a storm themselves.

Wait a minute…I think I recognize that tumbleweed of dark hair. The zombie she's with, not so much.

"*Niki*," I hiss at my tombstone-loving sister. "What are you doing here?"

"*Effie? Cooper?* Is that you?" she asks while scooping up my sweet pooches and stumbling this way. "I was just on a hot date with—"

She turns around and the zombie she was with seems to have disappeared as proficiently as an apparition.

Niki and I let out a short-lived scream at the same time.

Coop reaches for his gun.

"Where the heck did he go?" he shouts.

"Probably back to the crypt he crawled out of," Niki says matter-of-factly. "So what's next?" she asks, looking to the two of us. "I hear they have a pretty mean corn dog down at the fairgrounds. How about we hit that? I seemed to have worked up an appetite."

So much for having some alone time with the good detective.

But on another note, at least I didn't land him on the wrong side of the soil here at Honey Hollow Cemetery.

How's that for showing my true colors?

Although color me blue in the face come Tuesday if he's still breathing.

My Uncle Jimmy will make sure I'm not breathing either.

CHAPTER 17

$\mathcal{T}$he next morning I showed up at work bright and early. And as I strutted into the bakery, the scent of sugar and butter hit me like a one-two punch—and that's a one-two punch I will never complain about.

The customers kept us plenty busy straight through the morning and into the afternoon, and whenever we hit a lull, I shoved a glazed cruller into my mouth. But just a little after two the crowds die down and we can all catch our breath.

Lottie bounces to the counter holding a cake that looks a lot like a giant cream puff.

"Wow," I muse. "I think all of my cake dreams just came true."

"I sure hope so." Lottie laughs. "It's one of my new creations. I want you all to try it." She motions for Suze and Lily to come this way as well.

Carlotta is here, too, but she's way over by the door passing candy out of a cauldron to the cute little trick-or-treaters.

Halloween isn't for two days, but Main Street hosts a weeklong Honey *Hallow*-Haunt where schoolchildren are encouraged to dress in costume and go from business to business, in hopes their parents will find a new place to spend their money. Suffice it to say, no one leaves this bakery with just a couple of lollipops. Almost every one of those children's parents has bought boxes and boxes of sweet treats. So much so, we can hardly keep the shelves stocked.

"What is this?" Lily asks as both she and Suze take a well-deserved seat at the counter.

"Someone requested a cream cake for a Halloween birthday party and I needed to taste test it," Lottie tells her. "And you lucky ducks get to taste test it, too. It's basically pate choux dough with Bavarian cream filling. So it is essentially a giant cream puff, but I doubled the dough I would normally use for this size and the filling is a bit more like custard but stiffer."

She plates up a slice for each of us and we indulge at once.

I take a bite, expecting fireworks. And let me tell you, I got a full-blown pyrotechnic display in my mouth.

"Holy cannoli, Lottie. This is like biting into a cloud soaked in unicorn dreams," I cry with my mouth still full of creamy goodness.

Both Lily and Suze moan in approval as well.

The chime on the door jingles, and in comes another half a dozen little sugar fiends, all dressed up and ready to empty our candy stash faster than you can say *trick-or-treat*. They're so adorable all decked out like superheroes, a few princesses, and there are even a witch, a mermaid, and a ghost.

We watch as Carlotta begrudgingly hands out candy while muttering something about *kids these days and the lack of respect for their elders*. In her defense, the two littlest of the bunch just kicked her in the shin for the fun of it. And it was sort of fun to witness.

"Watch it, you little goblins," she growls. "Too much candy and your parents will have to peel you off the ceiling!"

Two of the mothers reach into their kid's plastic pumpkin buckets, scoop out a handful of candy, and land it right back in Carlotta's cauldron—twice as much as she gave to begin with.

It looks as if they won't be peeling anyone off the ceiling tonight.

Lottie shakes her head. "It's no wonder that cauldron is twice as full in the evening as it is in the morning." She shrugs as she heads our way. "So what are you ladies dressing up as for Halloween?" she asks the three of us while plopping next to Suze. "I'm thinking of going as a zombie bride. You know, the kind that's more interested in brains than bouquets. And I'm talking about those sugar-for-brains cupcakes."

"You've got sugar for brains, all right." Suze rolls her eyes. "I'll be passing out the candy at the B&B for your mother, Lottie." She turns my way. "You do realize the B&B is haunted. It's like Halloween there every night."

"I do," I say. And I also happen to know Suze plans on pocketing the full-size candy bars because I heard her telling one of the pastry chefs her nefarious chocolate-based plan earlier this week. I'm not so sure I blame her.

Lily nods. "I'm taking baby Levi trick-or-treating with Alex." Alex is her boyfriend, and also Suze's younger son. Little Levi's mother couldn't care less about Halloween or Levi himself, so Lily is essentially that boy's mama. "We're doing one of those family-themed costumes and going as cave people. Little Levi is going to be the cutest little caveman you ever did see." She holds her stomach and laughs as if envisioning it.

Suze smirks, shaking her head. "Ah, young love. Just wait until he's old enough to demand all the candy for himself. Then we'll see who's laughing."

Lily rolls her eyes. "Oh, he'll still be my little pumpkin, even if he does hoard all the candy. Besides, it's not like I won't sneak a few pieces for myself when he's not looking."

Suze raises a brow. "Now that's my kind of parenting. I used to steal the candy myself when my boys were that age."

"Alex told me all about it." Lily nods. "And once we're through trick-or-treating, Alex and I will continue with our roles as cavepeople right into the bedroom."

"And that was more than we needed to know." Lottie laughs.

Suze looks a little green around the gills just hearing it.

"How about you, Effie?" Lottie asks. "Got any big plans with Cooper?" She wiggles her shoulders as she says it. "That may or may not include a bedroom?"

"He didn't mention anything about Halloween when he picked the dogs up this morning. He'll probably be out patrolling the streets or something. It's Halloween," I say. "Something wicked is bound to happen."

"Yeah," Lily huffs with a silent laugh. "Something wicked will happen if you or Lottie is around. Face it, the two of you are a couple of walking, talking horror movies just waiting to happen."

"*Lily*." Lottie swats her with a towel as we gobble down our cream cake and Lottie doles us out each another slice. "Effie, you should go out and have fun even if it's not with Cooper. I bet all the men will want to glom onto you. That will teach Coop a lesson. And I bet he'll want to arrest every last one of them, too."

We share a laugh at that one.

Lily nudges Suze. "You should go out, too, Suze. Halloween is the perfect time to pick up men. All those costumes and masks, it's like a giant game of dress-up for adults."

Suze rolls her eyes at the thought. "You won't catch me chasing after any men in costume. I prefer my men unmasked so that I'm fully aware of what I'm getting into."

"Halloween is like the ultimate test for men," Lily says. "Can they handle a woman who's dressed to kill, both literally and figuratively?"

"I think I'll leave the killing to Lottie," Suze says just as the parents of those cute trick-or-treaters migrate in this direction.

Both Suze and Lily hit the registers, but as for me, I just finished up my shift.

Lottie leans my way as I take off my apron. "So how's the case going?"

But before I can answer, a tall, dark, and handsome

man gives her an embrace from behind.

"I'd like to know that myself," he says, offering me a dimpled grin.

It's Noah Fox—Homicide Detective Noah Fox to be exact.

Noah and Lottie share a little girl together, Lyla Nell. And she is as cute as a button. Lottie's mother watches her during the day at that haunted B&B of hers. And rumor has it, Lyla Nell just loves the ghosts.

Good thing Lottie is loaded. Something tells me she'll need the spare change for Lyla Nell's therapy bills.

"*Noah*," Lottie says, spinning in his arms and giving him a proper embrace. "What are you doing here?"

"I had some work in this direction and just finished up," he says. "Do you have time to get a quick bite at Mangias?"

"You bet," Lottie says, whipping off her apron. "Hey, Effie, you should come with us. I'm dying to hear what's going on with Sal's investigation."

Noah nods. "I'd love an update on the case as well. I was just meaning to talk to Cooper about it before I left the office. How about it? It's on me."

"Lunch at Mangias?" I bite down on a smile. Sure, Cooper asked me not to speak with Sergio Sorrentino, but he didn't ask me not to eat at Sergio's restaurant. And who am I to say no to both my boss and Cooper's boss by proxy? "You bet I'll join you. And I'll fill you in on every little thing I know."

With the exception of the fact that I need to shake Sergio Sorrentino down for a few missing details.

We hightail it out of the bakery for a slice of pizza and a side of justice.

CHAPTER 18

*N*oah holds open the door to Mangias for Lottie and me.

He's such a gentleman. I'm sure Cooper would have done the same if he was here, but since Cooper doesn't want me anywhere near this place, he might have asked me to turn around at gunpoint.

Speaking of gunpoint, my gun might be itching to make a point with that man, but I'm not so eager. And with my Halloween deadline looming large, Uncle Jimmy's henchmen will be looking to make one with me.

Hey? Maybe I should confess my conundrum to Cooper? Then we could scoop up our pooches and head for less mob-infested waters, like Alaska.

A visual of my fingers turning into icicles and snapping off flits through my mind and I usher the thought right back out along with all thoughts of frozen tundra.

But Mangias is far from a frozen tundra. In fact, it's darn right toasty in here. No sooner do we step inside than my nose is ambushed by the intoxicating scent of garlic and marinara.

Mangias is low-key casual dining with dark wood floors, matching wood furniture, and an ode to Sinatra blaring over the speakers. The Halloween décor has exploded inside with cobwebs in every nook and cranny and grinning jack-o'-lanterns on every table. And there are even spooky spiders dangling from the ceiling, threatening to drop down on unsuspecting diners at any moment.

The place is buzzing with chatter and laughter, and the clatter of dishes and the sizzle of the grill only add to the lively atmosphere. Witches' hats bob among the crowd and they're worn by both staff and patrons alike, adding to the festive chaos.

It's like stepping into a haunted Italian villa, complete with spooky ambiance and the world's best pizza.

"Boy, this place is packed," Lottie says as she cranes her neck into the crowd. "I don't think there's a single place for us to sit."

"Even the bar is packed solid. Nothing but monsters, ghouls, and witches as far as the eye can see," Noah grunts. "I guess we could get our food to go."

I crane my neck into the crowd as well and my heart skips a beat as I spot an all too familiar brunette seated at a table with none other than Sergio Sorrentino, the exact suspect I've been itching to shake down next.

"Or we can join my sister." I practically spit out the words because I'm not too thrilled with whatever she thinks she's doing.

Although, let's face it, I should be kissing her size sevens.

How does she always seem to entangle herself in my cases?

An ironic laugh thumps through me because I have a feeling Cooper has said those exact same words about me. And I know for a fact that Noah has said them when it comes to Lottie, too.

I lead the way, navigating us through the crowd and narrowly missing a baked rigatoni to the face in the process.

There they sit, heads bent together as they laugh and plot about who knows what, oblivious to the storm brewing inside me. Niki is dressed as a gypsy, a sultry vixen with far too much faux jewelry and not enough clothes to cover up her two best assets.

Sergio looks a little rough around the edges with his dark hair slightly mussed (most likely my sister's doing), his dark eyes filled with lust (definitely my sister's doing), and his hands rubbing her arms as if a cold front were about to push through.

That last part would be his doing, but if my sister has her way, he'll be doing it all night long.

What can I say? She might be dressed as a gypsy, but she'll always be a hussy at heart.

"Mind if we join you?" I ask as I pull out a seat and Noah and Lottie do the same.

"*Sergio.*" Noah shakes the man's hand before falling in his seat. "Great to see you. Hope you don't mind if we crash the party."

"For you, there's always a seat at my table." He laughs. "You, too, Lottie." He nods my way. "And who may I ask is this lovely lady?"

"My sister," Niki snips, and by the look on her face, there's a homicide she suddenly wants to commit.

"Nice to meet you," he says, offering me a hand. "Sergio Sorrentino. Welcome to my pizza paradise."

"Oh, I'm a frequent flyer at your pizza paradise," I say. "In fact, between your paradise and Lottie's bakery, my jeans seem to be shrinking in the wash."

He belts out a good-natured laugh. "I have the same problem."

"And she's funny, too," Niki deadpans while shooting me a look that says she'll be pointing her weapon at me next. Not that Niki has a weapon, but she wouldn't be above borrowing mine. My shoes, clothes, dogs, and a couple of odd boyfriends can attest to that.

A waitress dressed as a mummy comes by with lots of marinara sauce splotched all over those strips of linen covering her and it's a disconcerting look.

We put in our orders—lots of pizza, extra garlic bread-sticks, and a half sheet of lasagna. We're no fools.

"So Sergio…" Lottie leans his way. "I have to ask what you think of the new Italian place that just opened on the lake."

And just like that, the investigation is back on the table.

CHAPTER 19

*W*ow. Not only did Noah offer to pay for my meal when he threw out the invite, but Lottie is shaking down my suspect for me right here at Mangias.

"The Tavern of Terror?" Sergio grunts at the mention of it. "I've seen it. I know the clowns that opened its doors. God rest Sal Marino's soul." He makes the sign of the cross and shrugs.

I wonder what that shrug was for?

Maybe he realizes that he shouldn't be dragging the Man Upstairs into this, seeing that he's the one that pulled the trigger. Or maybe he's sorry he pulled the trigger and he was trying to shrug off the guilt he feels?

"So who owns it now?" Noah asks just as the bread-sticks are delivered and we all arm ourselves with the delectable delight. They're bathed in olive oil, sprinkled with just the right amount of garlic salt, and have that just-out-of-the-oven crunch before you get to the warm doughy middle.

If I ever get married, I don't need a bouquet of flowers. Give me a bouquet of garlic breadsticks from Mangias instead.

"Johnny the Meatball." Sergio rolls his eyes. "But make no mistake about it, that tramp he's seeing is the real boss of the joint."

Both Niki and I gasp at the Lazzari slight.

Good thing Cooper isn't here or bullets would be flying. Sure, Naomi got away with it, but she's a girl.

I have a feeling Sergio here would be toes up in the morgue before sundown.

"Tell me more," Noah says and I shake my head in awe. It's obvious he's a better detective than I am. Cooper? Not so much.

"Yeah," Lottie says. "Why the tramp comment?" I can tell she's a little peeved at the slight. Any woman on the planet can count on Lottie to have their back, even the trampiest woman of them all. Cooper's little sister.

"Sorry for the language." Sergio shrugs again and I'm starting to think it's a tick. "But the woman has been around the block. She's well known for her temper, too. And when she finally did settle down—twice—both husbands wound up dead with a bullet to their back."

"They don't call her Loretta the Black Widow Lazzari for nothing," Niki adds and I shoot her a look for contributing to the Loretta bashing.

"A bullet to their backs?" I shudder. She's a better shot than I am. Although if we're talking close range, the heat between our skills is still up in the air. "But she wasn't arrested," I point out. "She must be innocent."

Sergio is back to averting his eyes. "Her brother's a cop.

Sorry, Noah, but I know how things work. I live in the real world. The woman has gotten away with murder, not once but twice. I wouldn't dare cross her. But I'm guessing there's a Marino brother in the morgue who did."

Niki and I are right back to gasping.

Not only did Sergio call Loretta a tramp in mixed company, but he accused her of a record *three* murders— that includes the newly deceased whose case is quickly coming to a Lazzari finish. And I don't mean Cooper.

Lottie inches back. "Why in the world would she want Sal dead? The other two I can understand. I'm a married woman."

"Can I tell Everett you said that?" Noah is quick to ask. He's still got the hots for her, so I'm pretty sure she'd get a free pass from the homicide department, too.

And with my occupation, that's another reason I need to get in bed with Cooper, proverbially speaking. Although literally wouldn't be a bad idea either.

"No way." Lottie laughs. "And that's not what I mean. I mean, I get it, relationships can be tough. But why would Loretta want Sal dead? In the middle of a grand opening? And isn't she seeing his brother?"

I shake my head at Lottie in amazement. Why am I wasting my time with Niki, Aunt Cat, and Carlotta?

Clearly, the one I should be dragging to my shakedowns is Lottie and her boy toy with the badge. But then, Lottie has solved so many homicide cases herself, she's practically gone pro, too.

Sergio sighs. "Rumor has it, she was seeing both Marino brothers."

This time the entire table, sans Sergio, gasps.

"*Both* brothers?" Niki's jaw goes slack. "I wonder if she teaches a course on how to make men crawl all over you."

"*Niki.*" I reprimand her with a look for even going there.

"What?" she balks. "I'd pay cash money to have a few romantic entanglements myself."

"Entangled is the right word," Sergio says. "Sal was married. Poor Morella is a widow now. And there's not a soul in Honey Hollow who thinks she pulled the trigger."

A thought comes to me. "But what if she did? Word on the street is that Sal was cheating on her." That would have come straight from Loretta Lazzari's mouth on the night of the murder—and was given straight to the deceased. My eyes widen with fright at yet another terrifying prospect before he can ever answer.

"Yeah, he was a cheat." Sergio shrugs again as if it weren't all that big a deal.

I'm not exactly in the guy's fan club anymore. Although Niki still looks like a smitten kitten.

She would.

"What were you doing there that night?" Lottie asks unabashedly with the harbinger of a threat in her voice.

I really do like her.

Whoa—back up. Didn't Loretta say she was besties with Morella? And apparently, Loretta knows her way around a revolver or two?

And rumor has it, her brother has let her off the hook a time or two.

Is that why she's not on Cooper's suspect list? Does he know she's guilty?

I gasp all on my own.

Someone shouts for Sergio from the kitchen and tells

him to get off his culo—Italian for backside. And Niki chitters like a chipmunk just hearing it.

"Let's just say I was there checking out the competition," he says, answering Lottie's question as he rises to his feet. "I wasn't necessarily invited, but someone there owed me something." He snarls out the window. "Enjoy the meal. It's on me."

"Sweet. Thank you," Noah says as Sergio takes off.

The pizza and lasagna are delivered and we dive in, forgetting all about the dead sausage in the morgue.

Priorities.

Once we're done, we grab our stomachs and moan in unison.

"I'm so full, I don't think I'll eat for a week," I say.

"Sure you will," Niki says. "Tomorrow night is Sunday dinner. If you don't eat, Mom won't speak to you until Christmas."

"Are you trying to threaten me or encourage me?"

She shrugs in the same manner Sergio did. It must be catching.

"Suit yourself," she says. "But Cooper will be there regardless. He said he wouldn't miss it for the world."

"When did he say that?" I squawk.

"When I threw out the invite this morning."

"Wonderful."

Cooper is coming to dinner, and he's going to meet my entire family.

I think I just added another target to my hit list—my sister.

CHAPTER 20

*S*unday shows up faster than a groom at a midnight wedding in the middle of a graveyard.

People don't really get married that way, do they? Come to think of it, that's probably how I'll get married someday —to a reanimated corpse, seeing that I'm about to crest thirty and never had a man shove a sparkling rock onto any of my fingers. My toes haven't done so well for themselves either.

And speaking of potential husbands, Cooper sent me a message saying he'd meet me at my mother's with the pooches in tow.

It's going to be a circus, all right. And I have Niki to thank for this.

Grimstone Heights is my next exit. It's the cozy little town I grew up in. If you can call a high crime rate, drug rate, and dropout rate cozy. It was always referred to as *Little Leeds*. Not a compliment then, and certainly not one now. Leeds is known as the armpit of Vermont for a good reason.

The houses in Grimstone Heights are decorated to the spooky hilt, with each front lawn looking more gruesome than the last.

Back in Honey Hollow, it's mostly fall leaves, pumpkins, and inflatable ghosts that rule the roost. But here in Grimstone, we're talking Grim Reaper with ten bloody corpses, an entire army of skeletons, and every other lawn has transformed into a cemetery.

It takes less than two minutes to glide into my parents' neighborhood, where each house is smushed next to the last and a row of apartment complexes that sprang up across the street in recent years have turned the parking situation into a bona fide nightmare. But luckily, my parents converted half their front lawn into an extension of the driveway a few years back.

My mother figured we'd never visit if we had to park six blocks away, and she was right. My brother, Nico, got mugged one night doing just that. And my sister, Serafina, once had all four of her tires slashed when she parked in the alley—another no-no in this neighborhood. If you think the sidewalks are mean, the alley is where they train felons for a stint in prison.

Just a few years back there was a shooting at the liquor store down the block between rival gangs that left six people wounded. I've often said that you need a Kevlar vest just walking from the car to the house.

Speaking of cars or *trucks* as it were, no sooner do I jump out of my car than I spot Cooper walking up the street with two cute furry faces that look more than happy to see me.

"Babies," I shout as I kneel down and they rush over licking my face silly. "Are you ready to see Grandma?"

I'll admit, my parents weren't so thrilled with the way I let Watson run wild around their place the first time we visited. They grew up with a yard dog, but I've got to give them credit, they seem to be warming up to the idea.

"As long as you don't break any of her Capodimonte, you might be invited back." I jump to my feet and shrug at Cooper. "My mother likes to collect pricey figurines."

He nods, looking handsome enough to set the entire town on fire. "Same with mine."

He scoops me close and lands a warm kiss on my lips.

"Careful," I say. "If my father is watching from the window, he might be moved to load his gun."

He sighs toward the house. "Don't worry, I came packing heat myself."

"You sure you want to do this? You're a Lazzari coming in hot into Canelli territory."

"I've never backed down from a challenge. I'm certainly not going to start now."

"You talk a big game, but let's take what happens inside minute by minute. I think we should have a code word for a quick escape. How about *spaghetti?*"

He frowns and looks that much more lethally handsome. It's so unfair that I have to share him with my family tonight.

"How about *trick-or-treat?*" he offers. "Odds are good she's serving spaghetti."

"It's like you know my mother."

"I don't. But I know mine and I have a feeling they're not all that different."

And judging by that wry smile on his face, it's not necessarily a good thing.

We head up the porch and I give a brisk knock before letting myself in, and the first thing that hits me is the scent of roasted garlic and my mother's slow-cooked gravy, aka marinara sauce.

The second thing that hits me is the fact the living room has the table in it with its extension protruding out of it—something only reserved for special guests on Christmas Eve and Easter. A white lace tablecloth is stretched to capacity, overlaid with a sheet of clear glossy vinyl to protect it from the fury to come once we start eating. And instead of my mother's grocery store dinnerware that she's collected over the years, it looks as if we'll be eating off the good china, and that alone makes me want to shout *trick-or-treat*.

"They're here," Niki belts out, and within seconds my father, mother, sisters, and brothers swiftly assemble with military precision, forming a united front against the perceived threat of a Lazzari in their presence. It looks more like an imminent clash is about to take place rather than a Sunday dinner.

I have a feeling the Canelli-Lazzari turf war just spilled out into my mother's living room.

CHAPTER 21

"*W*hat's all the fuss?" a tiny voice shouts from the kitchen and out staggers Nona Jo, all four feet nine inches, with that gray mop of hair of hers teased into a beehive. A beehive you can see through right to her scalp, but a beehive, nonetheless.

It's Sunday dinner and Cooper is making quite the entrance as my family does its best to give him the stink eye. Thankfully, Nona Jo is here to talk some sense into them—I hope.

Nona Jo is as round as she is tall, but she packs a mighty punch with her words. She's one feisty broad I wouldn't want to meet up with in any alley, and certainly not the alleys around here.

"Is this him?" She breaks through the barrier between my father and mother and waddles over. "Is this the man who's going to finally give me the great-grandchildren I've been waiting for?" She pulls her glasses out of her bra and slides them on. "Good going, Effie. He's a hot one." She reaches up and gives Coop's cheek a pinch. "Sure you're a

Lazzari," she tells him with a slap. "But you've got the body, the face, and more importantly, the hair of a god. I have a feeling your good genes mixed with Effie's good genes are going to produce a superior race of Italians. And who knows? A Lazzari Canelli wedding might even be one to stop the turf war that's been going on for ages. It's about time we have peace in Little Italy, and it's you two who are going to bring it."

She says that last bit like a threat.

"Now where's my Watson?" she asks as both Watson and Spooky queue up for some Nona Jo loving and boy does she ever bring it. I'm not sure who's licking whose face more.

"Cooper, meet the family," I say. "You've already met my sneaky sister, Niki." I take a moment to glare at her. "The cutie next to her is my older sister, Seraphina. She works at the bookstore across the street from Lottie's bakery. She's got a steady Eddie and she's practically hitched."

Seraphina shoots me a look. "That steady Eddie of mine can be kicked to the curb at any moment. He's never so much as talked about rings." A devilish grin glides on her face as she offers Cooper a hand. "So nice to meet you," she purrs and now I'm glaring at *both* of my sisters.

Seraphina is cute as a button, same dark hair, same dark eyes as the rest of us. But she's hardwired to be a little Miss Priss, and that's probably why she's been the golden child for as long as I can remember.

My brothers are up next.

"My brother, Luciano, the baby. He works masonry with my pops." Cooper pauses to shake his hand and Luciano looks as if he's already plotting where to bury

Cooper's body. Probably under a pile of wet cement. "And the one with all the facial fur on the end is Nico, Niki's twin. He owns and runs the Last Call Lounge." Our Uncle Vito left it to him in his will, but I leave that part out. No one works harder than Nico and I'd hate for Cooper to get the wrong impression of him.

"The Last Call?" Cooper tips his head as he looks at my brother. "I was there just last week."

"You were?" I squawk as the two of them shake hands.

"They've got great wings," Coop says and Nico gives a furtive nod.

"You bet we do, buddy," Nico practically sings.

Buddy? At least Nico's not ready to bury him.

"Come around again sometime," Nico says like a dare. "It'll make it easier for me to keep an eye on you. Just remember, anyone who hurts one of my sisters is only going to hurt themselves." He crosses his arms, and his biceps turn into boulders as they stretch his T-shirt to capacity.

On second thought, he'd be more than happy to bury Cooper.

I glance to my parents, who still haven't taken their eyes off of him. Here goes nothing.

"Cooper, this is my mother, Renata. She works part-time at her sister's salon, the Hairway to Heaven." Mom looks like me plus thirty years. She dyes her graying locks jet black and wears it in the same beehive as her mother-in-law. And tonight she's donned her crisp white Battenberg lace apron—one I know for a fact she didn't cook a single dish with. I can tell she's rolling out the red carpet for Coop.

Mom loves bowling and booze, but Cooper can figure that stuff out later. Apparently, we've got some procreating to get to first.

"A pleasure to meet you," Cooper says as he carefully shakes her hand.

"*Please*, call me Mom."

I roll my eyes at that one. "Trick-or-treat?" I ask Coop in the event he's planning his exit.

He shakes his head. "Not even close."

Suit yourself.

"And this would be my pops," I say, giving my daddy a hug, but that stone-cold expression he's been wearing since we walked through the door only galvanizes itself. "He's known as Big Tom, but you can call him Dad," I tease.

"Big Tom works," Dad says, shoving a hand in Cooper's direction. Dad is tall, large, and more or less a giant teddy bear with his swath of gray hair, warm smile, and chubby cheeks that I still love to snuggle up to.

"Nice to meet you, Big Tom," Cooper says sincerely. "My dad goes by Scary Santino. He's got a scar that stretches across half his face that he got riding his bike as a teenager."

"You're Santino's kid?" Dad's eyes widen as large as Mom's meatballs. "We used to pal around when we were kids ourselves. Wait a minute." He straightens. "I was with him when he got that scar. We just stole a pack of cigarettes from the liquor store and tried our best to hightail it out of there." He points a finger my way, then zooms to my siblings. "Just because I did it doesn't mean you can. Nobody breaks the law in this family. Not anymore," he mutters. "I can't believe you're Santino's kid." A goofy grin rides up his face as he takes in Cooper. "We hung out quite a bit back in the day. But then we let all that turf war stuff get in the way. I'm real sorry about that, too. Tell your dad Tommy says hello."

"*Aww*, Tommy?" I coo just as Nona Jo belts out a whistle.

"If we keep this up, we're going to starve the poor guy out of the house," Nona Jo calls out so loud they heard us back in Honey Hollow. "A man's stomach is the key to his heart." She wags a crooked finger in my face. "You keep him well-fed, and he'll never stray far from home." She gives Cooper a pointed look. "An Italian wife who doesn't feed her husband risks losing him to a rival cook. And in our family, that's a fate worse than death."

"And on that note"—Dad pats his stomach—"mangia."

We quickly flock toward the table. The men take a seat while my sisters and I help my mother and Nona bring out about twenty different dishes.

Tonight, we eat like kings—round and happy Italian kings to be exact.

We've got my mother's homemade lasagna taking center stage with its layers of pasta, savory meat sauce, and gooey cheese melting in my mouth with every bite.

Next to it sits a steaming dish of chicken Parmesan, golden and crispy on the outside, tender and flavorful on the inside.

There's osso buco, Veal Saltimbocca, baked ziti, stuffed shells, mostaccioli and gravy, along with meatballs the size of my head. And let's not forget the creamy risotto with their perfectly cooked grains mingling with Parmesan cheese and sautéed mushrooms. A platter of bruschetta, topped with juicy tomatoes and fragrant basil, and then drizzled with balsamic glaze. And, of course, no Italian meal would be complete without a basket of warm, crusty bread to mop up every last drop of sauce.

We finish the culinary party off with my mother's famous tiramisu.

We've officially died and gone to Italian heaven.

Every last soul in the room moans with approval as we nearly empty out every last dish, and that's not a small feat considering the fact my mother made twice the feast she does on a regular Sunday.

Dad and my brother invite Cooper to watch the football game in the den. And my sisters and I join them while scrolling on our phones the entire time.

Watson and Spooky are cuddled up in Mom and Nona Jo's laps respectively, and this moment in time couldn't feel more Norman Rockwell if it wanted to—the Italian edition, of course.

It feels so normal.

So perfect.

It feels as if every last one of my dreams has come true.

The game ends and Dad nods to Cooper. "So what's the big case you're working on?"

"Sal Marino's murder," Coop offers up without hesitation. "I still have one more suspect to speak with and hopefully it'll wrap up quickly after that."

"Who's that?" Luciano asks, stealing Spooky from Nona. Luciano is lucky he's cute or he'd be missing a limb by now.

"Sergio Sorrentino, part owner of Mangias," Coop says before looking my way. "I was thinking of taking you there. I figure we could split a pizza and quiz him on his whereabouts that night together."

"Effie already beat you to it. She nabbed him at Mangias," Niki offers up, and I do my best to stab her with my eyes. Is that a thing? I'm making it a thing. "He was at the Tavern of Terror that night. Effie told him she saw him having it out with the deceased. And then he said something about checking out the competition and that someone there owed him something."

Cooper lifts a brow my way.

"Lottie and Noah invited me to lunch." I shrug. "But if you want to take me to dinner at Mangias, I won't say no." I pat my stomach. "Except maybe tonight."

The room breaks out into a good-natured laugh, and soon we say goodnight to one and all.

Some way, somehow Cooper Knox Lazzari survived Sunday dinner at the Canellis, and nary a bullet was fired. Not yet anyway.

We leash up the dogs and head on out. I take Cooper by the hand and lead him around to the side where a magenta-colored bougainvillea is doing its best to eat half the house.

"Guess where we are?" I ask, wrapping my arms around him and he does the same—albeit his hands are dangerously lower on my backside, but I'm not complaining. In fact, I wiggle my hips a bit so they sink down lower still.

"The open grave where you're going to bury me?" He tweaks his brows, but that stone-cold expression makes me wonder if he's serious.

"I'll have you know this is the fun zone, aka the safe place where my family can't see us from the windows or the porch. I used to bring all my dates here so we could make out like there's no tomorrow and they'd live to tell the tale."

"I'm starting to think you really do care about me."

"Are you kidding? I don't share dogs with just anyone. Which reminds me, what are we going to do with Spooky?"

"We'll deal with him later," he says, landing a kiss just shy of my lips and backing away. "I've got something far more delicious on my mind."

"Why, Detective, whatever could that be?" I bat my lashes up at him as he swoops in again and touches his lips to mine. This time I grab him by the back of the neck and hold him hostage there.

We make out like teenagers and make out like there's no tomorrow—if only he'd live to tell the tale.

If only it wasn't me who had to pull the trigger.

CHAPTER 22

The night air crackles as darkness descends upon us, casting its spell of mystery over all of Honey Hollow.

It's officially Tuesday, which just so happens to be Halloween and the deadline for me to produce two corpses for my Uncle Jimmy, or come midnight, I'll turn into a corpse myself.

After a long day at the bakery passing out haunted treats for the last six hours, I packed up my pooches and headed over to the haunted house on the water to round out my day.

The sun is setting and the sky is lit up in shades of pink and purple. I sent Cooper a text and asked him to dinner. And he messaged back that he was already on his way.

The Tavern of Terror is pulsing with an eerie energy as I step onto the patio, now transformed into a makeshift graveyard.

The canopy of purple twinkle lights shimmer in the breeze as fog from dry ice swirls at our feet. The music is loud and perfectly spooky, and the scent of something delicious sizzling from the grill makes my olfactory senses sit up and beg for more. If that wasn't wicked enough, every now and again someone belts out the occasional blood-curdling scream from the haunted house behind me.

I say hello to Naomi's head on a platter as she passes me by. I really need to find out how she's doing that. It's not just the stuff that nightmares are made of, I'm thinking I can make a few bucks off a stunt like that, too.

But I'm not headless tonight. In fact, I'm decked out in my best vampire attire, complete with a flowing black cape and fake fangs that threaten to fall out every time I open my blood-red lips. Not to mention I've donned a pair of killer glittery heels in a shade of blood-red that threaten to break my neck with every step, or with my luck a hip or two.

Watson and Spooky, my faithful furry friends, are dressed as a vampire and a ghost, respectively, and their costumes seem to elicit a chuckle from all who pass us by.

I'm about to hunt down Loretta and say hello, or boo as it were, but before I can hunt and peck for the Black Widow in question, I spot a couple of witches I know all too well.

"You do realize you're supposed to wear a costume tonight," I tease as I come upon Aunt Cat and Carlotta.

They're dressed to the nines in matching witchy attire. Aunt Cat's pointed hat threatens to topple over with her every move, while Carlotta's broomstick fashioned out of twigs and branches adds an extra air of authenticity to her ensemble. Come to think of it, she's probably *too* authentic.

"Costumes are overrated," Aunt Cat quips while giving

my sweet pooches a scratch. "We're all about keeping it real." She gives me a once-over. "I thought vampires only came out at night."

"It'll be dark in less than six seconds," I counter. "Besides, I couldn't resist the chance to mingle with the monsters." And by monsters, I mean killers. I crane my neck into the blossoming crowd of costumed characters as if I knew the exact monster I was looking for.

Carlotta smirks. "Speaking of monsters, have you seen the lineup at the bar? I think I spotted Frankenstein and his bride making out in the corner."

I glance that way and gasp. "I recognize that demented bride. It's Niki!"

"Darn tootin' it is," Aunt Cat sniffs with pride. "I taught that girl all of her demented moves."

"And you got those moves by watching me." Carlotta pins a greedy grin to her face. "So how's the investigation going, Eff? Any new leads?"

I cast a quick glance around before responding. "Not much progress. But I'm hoping to speak with Cooper's sister tonight. I have a feeling she knows more than she's letting on."

Carlotta's gaze sharpens as she leans in close. "Loretta the Black Widow Lazzari seems like a prime suspect in this whole nightmare. How many husbands has she gone through now? She practically has a revolving door at the family crypt."

"She certainly had a motive, that's for sure. I mean, the guy was stepping out on her best friend. That's enough for any woman worth her bestie salt to pick up a weapon. But I'll need more than speculation to pin anything on her."

"True," Aunt Cat says with a sigh. "It'd be a heck of a lot easier if the deceased was another one of her dead husbands."

Carlotta shrugs. "Then Coop could turn his head the other way once again and file this as another cold case."

I make a face. "As much as I hate to admit it, that might be true."

We part ways, and I'm about to take my pooches and head over to Niki to make sure she's a willing participant in that lip-lock since ol' Frankie there seems to have one heck of a death grip on her when I stumble upon an odd sight that stops me dead in my tracks.

There in the midst of the Halloween chaos stands none other than the Black Widow herself, decked out in a little red dress that screams danger and poor taste. It's low-cut down the front, high-cut up the back, and she has enough hot pink gems and pearls roped around her neck to fill a treasure chest. She's donned the pointy horns once again, along with the pointy tail, and looks just as devilish as the night I met her.

But what catches my eye even more is the scene unfolding before me.

Trick-or-treat, things are about to get scary.

CHAPTER 23

Standing by the railing near the lake, Loretta stands pointing a sharp red fingernail at a woman dressed as a naughty version of Snow White.

I scoot that way and duck behind a tombstone as I tip my ear their way. The tension crackles in the air around them, and each word is a dagger aimed at the other's heart as the accusations and the expletives go flying.

"Now why would I do that?" Loretta bites the air between them. "You're my best friend."

Her best friend? I pull the pooches in close, and lucky for all three of us someone dropped a couple of breadsticks and the dogs make quick work of it.

I take a closer look at the woman Loretta is handing a new one. That naughty Snow White must be the newest widow in town, poor Morella.

"Don't play dumb with me." Morella pokes a finger in Loretta's pillowy chest. "I know about your little trysts with my husband. You think you can just waltz into my territory and steal him away?"

ADDISON MOORE

I suck in a quick breath and inhale enough dry ice to freeze-dry my lungs. I do my best to cough it right back out and a plume of smoke expels from me.

"Your husband?" Loretta belts out a dark laugh. "Please, sweetheart, I had better things to do than waste my time with a two-timing loser like him. Maybe if you would have kept him on a tighter leash, he wouldn't have been sniffing around other women."

How dare she! The man is dead. Isn't the woman suffering enough?

"How dare you!" Morella echoes my sentiment and both Watson and Spooky give a soft woof in agreement. "I saw the way you were looking at him. And I saw the way he was looking at you, too. You thought you could just get in his face with your fancy clothes and your glossy smile and steal him away from me?"

"Oh, honey, I don't have to steal anyone. They come to me willingly."

I suck in another quick breath and so does Morella.

Loretta shakes her head. "But if you're looking for someone to blame for the marital problems you had, you might want to take a long, hard look in the mirror."

"You're nothing but a homewrecking harlot, Lazzari. Mark my words, I'll make sure you're twice as miserable as I am."

"Oh, I'm shaking in my stilettos, Mo. But if you want to play dirty, I can play dirty, too. Just remember, I never lose."

The slutty Snow White stomps off and I shake my head at Cooper's little sister. What in the world is she thinking, talking to her bestie like that? And at a time like this.

"I knew it," Loretta cries softly as she pounds her fists against the railing. "I knew if she found out it would ruin everything between us." She drops her chin to her chest and openly sobs as darkness covers all of Honey Hollow.

And just like that, I know exactly why she wanted Sal the Sausage dead.

Although a lot of good it did her. Her sins have been exposed.

But I'm not interested in Loretta's sins. I'm interested in the truth.

I tug Watson and Spooky in her direction and land in front of her just as the moon begins to glisten over the lake.

"Hey, Loretta." I offer a forlorn smile and she does a double take my way before glaring at me. "Are you okay?"

"It's none of your business." She reaches down and scoops up Spooky in haste before dropping a kiss to his furry little head and the poor guy squeals and wiggles as if she's about to toss him into the deep end of Honey Lake. And knowing her dark history with men, she just might.

"I heard what you said. Or more to the point, what she accused you of. Were you having an affair with Sal? While dating Johnny?" My eyes nearly bug out at the prospect. I've done some low things in my life, but that's low even for a devil like her.

She sniffs toward the lake. "It's not my fault. He kept plying me with limoncellos at his house one night after dinner. Johnny was with us at first. The three of us got together to discuss the opening of this place. We wanted to really stick it to the owners of Mangias. The Marinos and the Sorrentinos hate each other as much as the Lazzaris and the Canellis hate each other. Sal and Johnny were determined to put them out of business. Sal and Johnny argued about where they were getting their funding from. And Sal didn't like where Johnny was getting his half of the money. Johnny said that Sal was going to get the funds from his mystery lender over his dead body.

"Anyway, Morella was supposed to be there that night, too, but she had to work late at her shop. Johnny got called away to Leeds because he had a big dumb idea to procure a loan for this place from some dicey mobster."

Both Watson and Spooky turn their furry faces my way as if to ask the obvious.

And yes, I bet that dicey mobster was my uncle. And I also bet Johnny's failure to pay back the loan has a lot to do with why I have a bullet in my purse with Johnny's name on it.

Oh, for Pete's sake, this place hasn't been open for two weeks. Can't my uncle give the guy some slack? Like until Christmas? But then, I'll be dead by midnight because of Johnny's big dumb idea to borrow money he could never repay from a dicey mobster. Obviously, I won't be around for Christmas either if I don't take care of business.

"So you just slept with the guy once your boyfriend took off for dicey pastures?" I ask.

Loretta cuts an icy glance at the water. "Sal had to come up with half the money and he did, but he wouldn't tell us where it was coming from. I just had to find out where Sal and Morella came up with a quarter of a million dollars. They weren't wealthy, so while I downed the limoncellos, I was pumping him full of whiskey."

"Now there's a strategy. Get two people three sheets to

the wind via hard liquor and see who gets to their endgame first. I'm guessing it was him."

She nods as tears stream down her face. "I'll admit, I was weak and drunk. And to be honest, Sal looks a lot like Johnny with the lights out. I slept with my best friend's brother, and to make things worse, when Johnny came back he found me half-dressed. He asked for answers and I lied. But he knew. I could see it on his face."

"Is that why you did it?" I ask softly and both Watson and Spooky whimper. "Is that why you pulled the trigger and pumped Sal full of bullets?"

She inches back. "Are you insane? After my last two husbands were gunned down and I was accused of doing the dark deeds, I got rid of all my weapons. The last thing I need is for people to think I'm some sort of unhinged hit woman."

Hey, I resemble that remark.

And resemble it I do.

"I didn't kill him." She shivers as she holds Spooky tight. "But I found him out in the alley." She closes her eyes a moment too long. "I ran off to get help, but Coop had already discovered the body by then. There isn't a better detective in all of Vermont than my big brother."

Technically, it was me who found the body, but I leave the little macabre detail out of it for now.

She nods my way as she lands Spooky in my arms. "And I'm sure my big brother will track down Sal's killer, too."

"Morella wouldn't by chance own a gun, would she?" I cringe as I ask because that question just might get *me* thrown into the lake.

"Nope. Mo wouldn't hurt a fly. But if she was going to

kill anyone, it would be me." She sniffs once again before taking off.

"Wait a minute," I mutter to myself as I scoop up Watson, too. "She never did say who Sal borrowed his half of the money from."

That night at Mangias blinks through my mind and my eyes spring wide.

Loretta also mentioned that Johnny said Sal was going to get the funds from his mystery lender over his dead body. Or was it over *Sal's* dead body?

I glance up at the haunted house before me as the screams begin to intensify.

I have a feeling I know who the killer is, and just my luck, he's next on my hit list.

It's time to shake down the meatball one last time. Something tells me this is going to be the scariest Halloween night that Honey Hollow has ever seen.

CHAPTER 24

I stumble over to the haunted house here at the Tavern of Terror as Halloween night begins to hit its crescendo.

There's still no sign of Coop, but I've got a killer to hunt down and maybe kill one of my targets if I play my uncle's cards right. And speaking of kill, I've got a bullet earmarked for poor Coop, too.

I push the homicidal thought out of my mind for now. I've got until midnight to deal with that. I'm sort of a twisted Cinderella that way.

The back entry to the house of horrors is dimly lit with a plethora of spiderwebs and skeletons to traverse as I head deeper inside. I'm about to inspect every ghoulish nook and cranny this haunted hovel has to offer when I spot Naomi walking in this direction, her head on a platter—a look I'm becoming accustomed to when it comes to my nemesis.

"Naomi." I jump in front of her and note that her head is adorned with a crown of fun-size candy bars, so I scoop a few up with the hand I'm holding Watson with and shove them into the pocket of my cape. Yes, my cape has pockets, and that's exactly why I'll be reprising this look until spring. Those vampire fashion designers really do understand a woman's needs. I scoop up another handful for the sake of balancing out my costume. Besides, everyone knows food is fuel, and chocolate is basically nuclear energy when it comes to me. "Do you know where I can find Johnny?" I ask, peeling open a fun-size Snickers and popping it into my mouth posthaste.

"I think so." Naomi shrugs, and believe me when I tell you a shrug without a head to go with it is a disconcerting look. "The guy who was supposed to play the part of the ax murderer didn't show up, so Johnny had to cover. He's upstairs, third nightmare on the right," she shouts before leading a pack of spooky patrons out onto the patio.

"An ax murderer? Just my luck," I mutter to Watson and Spooky as the three of us shiver and quiver our way through the ever-darkening hall and over to the stairwell.

With every step I take, the air grows thick with an eerie chill, and the dim lighting casts ominous shadows across the walls. Ghoulish figures leap out from hidden alcoves, eliciting startled yelps from my pooches and me. So much for protecting me with their canine prowess.

My heart pounds in my chest as I navigate through the maze of horrors, and every creak of the floorboards, every distant moan sends a shiver down my spine—and more than a couple of screams from my lips.

I venture deeper into the haunted house, and with each step, the atmosphere becomes increasingly sinister. The corridors are narrow. The decrepit wallpaper is peeling.

And it all creates a creepy backdrop for the horrors that lurk within—lots and lots of horrors.

Confession: I'm not so keen on Halloween. I'm specifically not so keen on Halloween while walking through a haunted house.

Cobwebs dangle from the ceiling, swaying in the faint breeze while flickering torches cast shadows across the uneven floor.

I traverse goblins, ghouls, and enough demented clowns to take over Congress before I hit the stairwell and fight my way upstream as an endless cache of screaming teenagers bypass me at the speed of light as they run in the opposite direction.

Instinctively, I realize that I should never go against the grain when it comes to a crowd shrieking in terror. But it's Halloween and we're in a haunted house. This is all makeup, smoke, and mirrors, right?

I'm about to crest the landing when I hear a deep voice shout my name from the ground floor.

"*Effie Canelli*," he thunders again. "Wait for me."

I turn around, half-afraid it's the Grim Reaper himself, but much to my relief, it's Cooper looking lean, mean, and far more delicious than the chocolate I stuffed into my cape. Come to think of it, I wouldn't mind stuffing him into my cape either.

"Fancy meeting you here," I say as he dots a kiss to my lips and takes Spooky from me.

"I'm sorry I'm late. But glad I get to join you for the adventure." He glowers at the top of the stairwell where the creepy music only seems to get louder and purple lights blink off and on in a spasm. "You sure you don't want to eat dinner first? I hear it's pretty gory up there. It might ruin your appetite."

"Have you met me?" I'd laugh, but I've met me. "Nothing can ruin my appetite," I say. Other than pumping a bullet into his back perhaps. And note I said *perhaps*. "Besides, I've got a hot date with an ax murderer. You can tag along if you like."

"A hot date, huh?" he muses as we climb the rest of the stairwell. "Good thing I'm packing heat. I'm not so keen on anyone dating the woman I'm destined to create a race of super Italians with."

"You laugh, but I'll have you know Nona Jo's predictions have come true time and time again. She has a one hundred percent prediction rate. The circus back in the old country tried to get her to join in on the traveling fun. They even said she could charge whatever rates she wanted for her sideshow act, but she had marinara on the stove, a bun in the oven—my father—and a husband to keep in line. I'm pretty sure she eschewed a fortune in the name of family."

"Family first has always been my motto as well," Coop says, lifting Spooky a notch as if he were toasting me with him.

"*Aww*," I coo.

Cooper really is perfect.

Such a pity he has to die.

I really should call my uncle. But first, there's the business of that ax murderer.

Cooper steps ahead and leads the way through the maze of horrors and I hook my free arm around him and bury my face in his shoulder as we traverse killer clowns, men with chainsaws, witches with flying monkeys, and the most terrifying creatures of all—haunted dolls.

"I think the ax murderer is up next," Cooper says as he points to a sign that reads, *beware of the lunatic lumberjack.*

"Wonderful," I whimper and Watson joins in with me. This is probably a good time to let Cooper in on the fact I'm about to accuse the lunatic in the room before us of murder. "Okay, Coop, there's probably something I need to tell you—" I start just as a group of teenagers runs out of the room screaming their heads off—and a couple of them called out for their mommies.

I'm starting to wish my mother was here, too. She might be diminutive in size, but that foot-tall beehive gives her an abundance of power.

Not only could she take down any lunatic with just one look, but her razor-sharp tongue could make a grown man cry. Just ask my father—and maybe Cooper if something should go severely wrong when I accuse the ax murderer of well, murder.

CHAPTER 25

*T*he room is decked out to look like a forest, alive with flashing red strobe lights, and the depth and width of the place seems to evade the principles of time and space.

"Wow," Cooper marvels as the fog begins to thicken. "It's as if we're really in the woods. This entire place is incredible. I'm not sure what kind of black magic they're using to pull this stuff off, but it's genuinely creepy."

"I've long suspected Naomi Turner was a powerful witch, and seeing that she can pull off the headless look and run this haunted hovel with her head on a platter proves it."

"Duly noted," he says.

If only my evening ended there. It would truly be the perfect night.

"*Trick-or-treat*," I call out with caution as the eerie mood music builds as we enter deeper into the haunted woods. "*Johnny Marino*, come out, come out, wherever you are!"

A loud thwack comes from our left and a giant ever-green falls this way, missing us by inches.

"*Geez*," Cooper growls as he pulls me out of harm's way. "They've got some real liability issues here. If they're not careful, someone might really get hurt."

"Someone's going to get hurt, all right," a deep voice rumbles, and out of the shadows steps Johnny the Meatball Marino wearing a ripped-up flannel and jeans, along with tall black boots and a dirty beanie pressed over his head. His facial scuff looks thicker than usual, and yet there's dirt smeared over his nose and cheeks to give him that I-chop-for-a-living look. "Hey, it's you." He nods to Cooper. "Sorry, Detective, but I've got an ax to grind tonight." He belts out a laugh. "How are you enjoying the show?"

"It's perfectly terrifying," Cooper says with a laugh. "This place is great. You should leave the attraction up all year."

"I was toying with the idea, but you know your sister. Once she vetoes something, it's hard to get your way."

Cooper offers an affable smile. "You really do care about her, don't you?"

"I'd kill for that girl," Johnny says, slinging his ax onto his shoulder as a glint of darkness flickers through his eyes.

"And you have, haven't you?" I say as my heart begins to race ten times as fast as it did with any of those fake monsters we've encountered. Okay, so maybe it pounded a little harder in the room with the creepy dolls, but who could blame me?

"Pardon?" Johnny squints my way as the lights continue to flicker around us.

145

"You heard me," I say. "Johnny, I know what you did and why you did it."

He inches back. His eyes flit to Cooper, then to the exit behind me.

Cooper shakes his head my way. "What's going on, Effie?"

"I think Johnny should tell us." I nod to the man, but the only thing he seems capable of doing is glaring at me as if he were about to find some place new to bury that ax. "Fine. I'll get the ball started. I heard you had a problem with how your brother was able to fund his share of this place."

Johnny's eyes expand and he shoots me a look. "So what if I did? He's dead. It's water under the bridge."

"What's going on?" Cooper loosens his hold on my waist and looks as if he's about to reach for his weapon.

"Johnny here didn't like that Sal borrowed money from Sergio," I tell him.

"I hate the entire Sorrentino clan," Johnny riots and swings his ax at the nearby trunk of a tree. The smell of whiskey emanates from his breath even at our vantage point. "Why he thought it was a good idea to go groveling to the enemy is beside me."

"You thought he was a traitor," I continue.

"Sal was a traitor," he riots and his eyes are red with rage.

"He betrayed you in another way, too, didn't he?" I go on. "With the woman you love."

"What?" Cooper snaps his neck my way. "What are you saying?"

"I'm saying that Sal the Sausage got your sister snockered up on limoncello and then he took advantage of her."

A riotous roar evicts from Johnny and he goes on a wild swinging spree with that ax of his.

Both Cooper and I put down our pooches but keep the leashes held tight. Cooper puts a hand over his weapon but doesn't quite remove it from its holster just yet. I'm no psychic, but I bet that's next.

"Back up," Coop shouts my way, but I take a step forward instead.

"Is that why you killed him?" I shout over Johnny's wild howls. "Is that why you sent Sal packing to the big haunted house in the sky?" I suppose it's the ultimate haunted house, but I'd venture to guess it's not nearly as gory or scary. That is, unless you end up in the hot place. Then it's sort of a haunted house twenty-four seven for all of eternity.

"*Yes*." Johnny jumps in front of me with such vigor the floor shakes beneath our feet. His eyes are bloodshot, his face glows as if his skin is on fire from the inside, and his rage is palpable. "I killed him because I *had* to. Not only did he disrespect me as a businessman by going to our enemy to build this place, but he disrespected me as a brother when he took my girl. Sal Marino was a traitor, and there's no room for a traitor in the Marino family no matter who he is. He's in a casket where he deserves to be and I'm the one who put him there." He swings his ax at the tree to his left and it falls over with a crash, sending the dogs into a barking tizzy.

"*Freeze*," Cooper shouts at the man while aiming his gun at him, but Johnny simply swings his ax at the weapon.

"I'm not going anywhere, Officer," Johnny shouts, and the next thing I know he snatches me by the wrist and lands the crook of his arm around my neck. "Sorry, Cooper. If I'm taking a road trip to Hell, she's coming with me."

"No can do," I squeak. "I hear the heat can be a real killer this time of year." I turn my head to the right and lift his arm right off of me. I dance backward, and in one quick move, I manage to dig my Glock out of my purse and point it at the lunatic in question.

In an odd turn of events, I'm actually facing both Johnny and Cooper, my weapon inadvertently pointed at the two of them.

My twin targets.

There's not another soul in the room as far as I can see, save for the dogs, and if I happened to take down my two intended hits, I'm sure they'd never tell. Although let's be honest, Watson would never forgive me for taking out his father. I don't think I could forgive myself either.

Cooper turns his head slightly, his eyes never leaving mine as if he knew what I was contemplating. He lowers his weapon and gives a slight nod my way as if daring me to do it.

A fresh bout of rage enlivens in me and it's all for my uncle, and maybe for myself, too, for getting stuck in such a Glock-shaped pickle.

"Don't just stand there," I shout to Cooper. "Arrest him."

Cooper goes to tackle the perp, but Johnny springs in my direction so I fire a shot and hit him in the hip, knocking him right to the floor.

While Cooper cuffs him and calls for help, I quickly put

away my gun and scoop up my sweet pooches and smooch their little faces, just thanking the Big Guy Upstairs they came away without a scratch.

I watch as Cooper shouts into his phone, and Johnny writhes while pinned beneath Cooper's knee as both of my targets are still alive and kicking.

My targets might be alive and kicking, but I don't think I'll be so lucky come midnight.

Soon enough, the sheriff's department swarms the place. Johnny is arrested and taken away by the EMTs, along with a few deputies to make sure he doesn't go anywhere. Not that he can with the bum hip I gave him.

Cooper and I follow them out to the front of the Tavern of Terror and watch as the ambulance takes off.

"You did good, Detective Canelli," he says, holding Spooky while I hold Watson tight as can be. "Next time give me a little warning and leave the shooting to me."

There won't be a next time, I want to say but don't have the gumption to.

"I've got news about Spooky." He frowns a bit as he says it. "Naomi let me know the owner called and was asking about him. He belongs to a very nice family who lives right here near Main Street. I let her know I'd return him as soon as I could. His name is Sparky, and it turns out he came from the same litter as Watson."

"I figured so," I say, giving the little cutie a scratch over the ears. "I'm really going to miss the little guy." The brownies he leaves in my front yard, not so much.

"I let the lady know where you work and that I hang out at the bakery a lot myself with Watson. She said she's going to set up some playdates for the two of them at the dog park."

"*Aw*, I love that." My heart melts just thinking about it. And then a visual of me lying dead in a casket takes over. Then another visual of Cooper falling in love with Sparky's mom, and suddenly I want to shove every candy bar in the world into my pie hole. But face it, there's not a candy bar in the universe that can fix what's wrong in my world.

"I'd better get going," Cooper says. "I've got a mountain of paperwork waiting for me and I want to book Johnny before the night is through. Try to keep out of trouble, would you?" He gently lifts my chin with his finger and steadies his eyes over mine. "For a second there tonight, I thought you were going to shoot me."

"For a second there tonight, I thought the same thing." I try to make it sound as if I were teasing, but it comes out like an apology. And I am sorry I ever entertained the idea, let alone trained a weapon on him.

Cooper gives me a deep, dark, delicious kiss before we part ways.

Watson and I say goodbye to Spooky and watch as the two of them take off.

After Cooper drops the pooch off at his forever home, he said he's headed straight for Ashford.

And I take off for Leeds.

If my uncle is about to do me in, I may as well make it easy for him. Or find a way to change his mind.

Whichever comes first.

CHAPTER 26

*H*alloween night has held many memories for me, mostly chocolate-filled, gluttonous memories where I eventually passed out in a sugar coma.

Although there was that one time with Timmy Jenks, where our braces locked and we spent the next few hours in the ER, but I push that nightmare out of my mind.

Tonight, on this Halloween night, I certainly made some new memories that I won't soon forget—that is, if I live past midnight.

Watson and I arrive at Red Satin Gentlemen's Club down in Leeds in record time. All the way here we were already missing Spooky something fierce. I'll have to contact his new owner in the morning about getting together at the dog park asap. Yet again, that is, if morning ever comes for me. And if it doesn't, Watson will most likely be missing me as well. Or at least he should. I do feed him.

I scoop up my furry fellow vampire of the night and we

151

duck inside the red-clad oasis with girls in various levels of undress parading around.

Both the men and women here tonight have some sort of costumes on, the lights are dim yet strobing, and lots of fog seems to be swirling around the joint. The music is far too loud and the men that are screaming sound as if they're experiencing pain far more than they are pleasure.

This is pretty much how I imagine it is in Hell.

Speaking of which, I'd better get down to the devil's lair. It's time to beg for mercy from the one devil that never gives it.

Watson whimpers as if he read my mind, and believe me I'm about to whimper, too—right after I finish groveling to my Uncle Jimmy.

We make our way through the dark hall in the back, down to the casino where the lights from the one-armed bandits are whirling and twirling. The place is packed tonight, and most of the people down here are in costumes as well.

The smoke swirling about is coming from cigars, and all of the blackjack and poker tables are brimming with bodies, most of them stony-faced men. The music is just as loud as upstairs but the scent of whiskey is thicker. As tempting as it is to shove a few quarters into a slot machine, I hang a left and navigate the labyrinth of hallways until I come upon one of Uncle Jimmy's faithful goons guarding his office.

I'm about to ask him to shoot me and make it quick, but he opens the door and leads me to a fate worse than death —my uncle.

Uncle Jimmy sits smoking a stogie and the smoke

veiling him makes him look even more like a mythological creature than he already does—not the pretty ones, but the big scary ones that everyone does their best to avoid. He's basically a villain in every iteration you can think of. And he's pretty good at it, too.

"You come bearing good news?" he asks, setting his cigar in an ashtray and motioning for me to hand Watson over.

I'll do no such thing. Instead, I set the pooch down on the desk and let Watson's free will determine where it will take him. And as my luck would have it, his free will sends him scampering for Jimmy.

"Sit, Bella," he instructs and both Watson and I land on our tushies before him. "Where'd you do the dirty deeds, and do we need a cleanup crew to take care of the bodies?"

I frown at the thought.

A cleanup crew is made up of about six to twelve of his men, depending on how gruesome the scene is. Rumor has it, within ten minutes they could have the slaughter grounds sterile enough to perform open heart surgery for the Pope.

I'm guessing the same could be said for this office once he takes care of me.

"Actually"—I lift a finger as a bevy of lies try to infiltrate my lips, but alas the truth wins out—"the scene of the crime was at the Tavern of Terror, an upstairs room where Johnny was dressed as a lumberjack. We had it out. He swung an ax my way and I shot him."

The truth does have a way of looking good if you omit certain details.

He blinks back. "Good work." There's a note of surprise

in his voice as if he didn't think I had it in me and I take umbrage with that. Not that I *did* have it in me, but still.

If either of us should believe in my executioner skills, it should be him. After all, he's doling out the big bucks for me to perform.

"So you got 'em both?" His brows furrow as his perplexity seems to grow. So much for believing in me.

"I shot Johnny in the hip. He confessed to killing his brother in front of Cooper—Detective Knox—Lazzari, and well, Cooper had to take off to process the guy. I guess you could say I missed my chance."

Uncle Jimmy rolls his eyes. "So they're both still breathing. But since Johnny is headed to prison and Sal is dead, it looks as if I'll get my investment back anyway."

"How do you figure?"

"When Johnny borrowed the cash, I had my lawyers write an addendum to the deed stating that should anything happen to him—prison included—I get the restaurant."

"You mean his share?" I tip my ear his way. "Sal had a widow. I guess you'll be in business with Morella Marino."

"Not true. Sal had messy financials. It was easier for Johnny to procure the place alone even though they were going to go in halves. It was a good guy agreement between brothers. I guess one of the brothers wasn't such a good guy. I respect Johnny for popping the traitor. I could see how he could get over the fact Sal borrowed money from the man they both hated. Borrowing money from your enemy can quickly turn into a heist if you never plan on paying them back. But sleeping with his wife? The guy signed his own death certificate when he pulled that off."

"Wait a minute." I jump in my seat. "You knew that Johnny killed Sal and *why!*"

His shoulders twitch. "He showed up in my office a few days back and confessed the whole thing. He wanted advice on how to avoid the detective that was breathing down his neck."

"That would be Cooper." I cringe.

I'm getting the feeling Cooper knew more than he was letting on, too. Let's hope that's all he's aware of.

"Which brings us to the next point of contention. The detective." Uncle Jimmy sighs. "I take it you've had more than a few opportunities alone with the guy to pop him into tomorrow."

Watson growls and I'm moved to do the same, but I'm already skating on thin ice as it is.

I could lie, but then lying to Uncle Jimmy is a lot like lying to the Big Guy Upstairs. There's no use. Uncle Jimmy already knows the truth.

"Yes." I sigh. "I had ample opportunity to land him in the morgue—which I didn't do. But if it means anything, I did manage to land him in a cemetery a few days back." Sure, it was during that ghoulish walking tour, but again with the truth, less is more.

He frowns my way. "Fess up, you didn't do it and the job has gone unfinished."

I hang my head on cue. "Go on. Make it quick. And don't let me suffer. You can tell my parents I moved to Alaska and maybe they won't suffer too much either."

"Look at me," he thunders and my eyes flit to his. "I had a very interesting visit yesterday from a certain someone who knew about the hit."

"The hit on Cooper?" I gasp. "Was it my ridiculous sister? Oh, please don't make me kill her, too. I mean, most of the time I *want* to, and believe me, it wouldn't even be a challenge, but I'm pretty sure she's harmless. Sure, she's a tattletale and she'll probably tell everyone that I'm a hit woman for hire for the biggest mobster around, but that's only because she's proud of me. And she might be an incessant gossip."

His furry brows swoop together. "No, it wasn't Nicolette." He's always referred to my sister by her formal name. On second thought, I think this is the first time he's referred to her at all.

"Was it Aunt Cat? Or that goofy friend of hers, *Carlotta?*"

Uncle Jimmy's right hand flies to his holster. "Call Carlotta goofy again and see what happens."

"Duly noted." I give an audible gulp. It's clear he still has the hots for her.

"But it wasn't either of them either, and it wasn't Cupertino himself. It was your nona."

"Nona Jo?" I squawk.

"She's the only nona you got living."

I give a furtive nod to affirm the fact.

"So what happened?" I ask with an entirely new level of fear rising in me.

"She let me know there's going to be a wedding." He glowers right at me. "That the detective is going to plant his Lazzari seed inside you and that you're going to have a thriving garden of children."

My mouth squares out at how graphic he felt he needed

to be. Come to think of it, he could just be repeating what Nona Jo told him. That's so her.

"She said she gave you her blessing," he roars as if the thought infuriated him. "Why didn't you tell me? I thought we were close. Do you know what kind of curse would have fallen upon me if you carried out my orders? It could have had the power to unravel my entire empire." He waves his hand at the rusted filing cabinet to his left. "I would have lost my footing to the Lazzaris. And the Canelli name would have been mud—worse than mud because no one would want to step in it in fear the curse would fall upon them, too." He shakes his head at me. "We're both lucky Nona Jo had the good sense to drop by."

Boy, I'll say.

Although the real lucky one around here is Cooper—and maybe me, seeing that I'll most likely live past midnight.

"But here's the caveat." He holds up a thick finger my way and I nod because there's always a caveat. "I don't care how many years go by. If the two of you split ways, I'll have one of my men take him out myself. But as long as the two of you are happy, he lives to see another Lazzari day."

Wonderful. Unbeknownst to Cooper, I'm the key to life.

"So now what?" I ask and immediately regret the words as they come from my mouth. I should have said thank you, grabbed the dog, and ran for Honey Hollow.

"Now you wait for your next assignment," he says, reaching down and opening a drawer on the right side of his desk before plunking down a wad of cash in front of me. "I'm paying you for both jobs. You got Johnny to pay me back—not with his life, but with something better, waterfront property in Honey Hollow. And you get to grow your garden of children with the detective. But you got to throw him, as far as your gig for me is concerned. I don't care how many secrets you want to spill during your little pillow talk sessions. This arrangement between the two of us isn't one of them. If he finds out, *I* take him out. Capiche?"

"Capiche," I say, snatching up the money, the dog, and what's left of my sanity. "Happy Halloween," I shout as I bolt out of his office, out of the casino, out of the armpit of Hell, and jump back into my car.

The devil may have had mercy on me, but it took an angel to convince him.

And that angel's name is Nona Jo.

$\mathcal{I}$t might be late on Halloween night, but I'm not headed back to Honey Hollow.

Instead, I stop off at an all-night donut shop and pick up a box of the best crullers you ever did see just this side of Lottie's bakery. Half vanilla glazed, half chocolate glazed.

In no time at all, Watson and I are striding into the Ashford County Sheriff's station.

Sure, I can't share the good news with Cooper that his head is off the chopping block, but I can share a box of donuts with him without having to pretend I'm not looking for an opportune time to send him into tomorrow.

Speaking of tomorrow, I might have to stop by Grimstone and hand Nona Jo a box of crullers as well. It's safe to say, I owe her big time—so does Cooper—and maybe our future children.

The sheriff's department is teeming with bodies. It's about an even split between drunken men and women in really bad costumes—we're talking trash bags with duct tape for the men and lots of fishnet stockings for the women. Either that or the sheriff's department has a run of serial killers and prostitutes. Come to think of it, it's probably the latter.

I spot Noah Fox up front and I head his way.

"Effie." He sheds a dimpled grin before giving Watson a pat. "What are the two of you doing here?"

"I thought I'd visit Coop and spread some carbohydrate-laden cheer," I say, opening the box. "They're not Lottie's, but they're still delicious. Take one," I offer and he promptly does.

"Thank you," he says, toasting me with the confection. "Coop's in his office. Tonight's a busy one. You know what they say, the freaks come out at night."

"And on *Halloween* night, you can double that," I say and we both share a quick laugh before parting ways.

Watson leads me straight to Cooper's office, his stomping grounds when he's not with me.

The door is ajar and I give a light knock before peering inside. "Hello?" I call out. It's dimly lit by a small lamp on his desk, but there's no sign of Cooper.

The office is big and has the potential to be bright when the overhead fluorescent lights are on full blast, but seeing they put out as much luminosity as the sun, I don't blame him for not turning them on.

I head in and land the donuts on his desk. I'm about to pull out my phone and let him know I'm here when I spot that suspect board in front of me.

Situated right behind Cooper's desk is a whiteboard that spans ten feet wide with pictures of all of the jobs I've been given from the time I took the job as a hitwoman for my uncle. I've seen it before. Cooper let me know a while back that it was his responsibility to track down the common factor that befell all of these men. He highly suspects there's a mob connection in there somewhere, and boy is he right.

I make my way around the desk to give it a gander and inspect all of the men with their names and locations of the maimings, since none of them resulted in death. I'll admit, it makes me chuckle. There's even a smidge of pride as I take it all in.

A photo in the upper right catches my eye and it's startlingly out of place. It's a picture of Cooper.

Why in the world would he put his own picture on the board? He's the investigator.

Unless...

Something soft and furry seems to be lining the board, and the closer I get I can see it's a series of strings, blue yarn to be exact, that's connecting all of the familiar faces dotting the board and they all lead to one central location in the middle.

I take a few steps in that direction, only to find a grainy-looking picture of a woman's face in the dead center of the melee.

And once the image comes into focus I gasp.

It's *me!*

Footfalls echo from behind and I turn to see Cooper standing there with his hands in his pockets.

He nods my way and offers a sober smile. "Happy Halloween."

My mouth falls open, but not a sound comes out.

Something tells me things are about to get very, *very* scary.

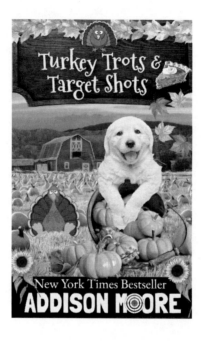

**Thank you so much for reading Double Double Recoil & Trouble. Be sure to grab the next book in the series —> Turkey Trots & Target Shots!

RECIPE

From the Kitchen of Effie Canelli

Easy-Peasy Cannoli Dip

Hey there! It's me, Effie. While I love cannolis from the bottom of my soul, I'm not such a fan of making the shells from scratch. So I came up with a way to have the best of both worlds! Create a dip with yummy filling and break up pieces of a sugar cone to dip into the deliciousness! It's not only easy, it's darn right heaven.

You're welcome!

Ingredients

1 1/2 cups whole milk ricotta cheese
1/2 cup powdered sugar, plus extra for dusting
1 teaspoon vanilla extract
1/4 cup mini chocolate chips, plus extra for garnish

Waffle cones or cinnamon sugar tortilla chips for dipping

Directions

In a mixing bowl, combine the ricotta cheese, powdered sugar, and vanilla extract. Stir until well combined and smooth.

Gently fold in the mini chocolate chips until evenly distributed throughout the mixture.

Transfer the cannoli dip to a serving bowl and sprinkle additional mini chocolate chips on top for garnish, if desired.

Serve the cannoli dip immediately with waffle cones or cinnamon sugar tortilla chips for dipping.

If desired, dust the top of the dip with powdered sugar for an extra touch of sweetness before serving. (I always desire.)

Enjoy this easy and delicious cannoli dip with all the flavors of traditional cannolis but without the hassle of making the shells from scratch! Woo-hoo!

BOOKS BY ADDISON MOORE

Cozy Mystery Series

Cruising Through Midlife:
Cruise Ship Cozy Mysteries

Brambleberry Bay Murder Club

Meow for Murder Mysteries

Country Cottage Mysteries

Murder in the Mix Mysteries

Hot Flash Homicides

Pain in the Assassin Mysteries

For a full list visit addisonmoore.com

ACKNOWLEDGMENTS

Big thanks to YOU the reader! I hope you had a wonderful time. I can't thank you enough for spending time in Honey Hollow with me. I hope you enjoyed Effie and all of her Honey Hollow peeps as much as I did. If you'd like to be in the know on upcoming releases, please be sure to follow me at **Bookbub** and **Amazon,** and sign up for my **newsletter.**

Thank you from the bottom of my heart for taking this wild roller coaster ride with me. I really do appreciate you!

A very big thank you to Kaila Eileen Turingan-Ramos, and Jodie Tarleton for being awesome.

A special thank you to my sweet betas Amy Barber and Margaret Lapointe for looking after the book with their amazing beautiful eyes.

A mighty BIG thank you to Paige Maroney Smith for being so amazing.

And last, but never least, thank you to Him who sits on the throne. Worthy is the Lamb! Glory and honor and power are yours. I owe you everything, Jesus.

ABOUT THE AUTHOR

Addison Moore is a *New York Times, USA Today,* and *Wall Street Journal* bestselling author who writes contemporary and paranormal romance. Her work has been featured in *Cosmopolitan* Magazine. Previously she worked as a therapist on a locked psychiatric unit for nearly a decade. She resides on the West Coast with her husband, four wonderful children, and two dogs where she eats too much chocolate and stays up way too late. When she's not writing, she's reading. Addison's Celestra Series has been optioned for film by **20th Century Fox.**

Made in United States
North Haven, CT
03 August 2024

55690795R00105